# Never Make Promises

## S.R. Burks

A NOCTURNA PRESS BOOK

Cover Design: Nocturna Press
Cover Art: Red Paint by Jag_cz | Fotolia.com

Nocturna Press
Independence, Missouri
www.NocturnaPress.com

ISBN-13 978-1-944673-24-6 (paperback)
ISBN-13: 978-1-944673-23-9 (e-book)

Library of Congress Control Number: 2018960412

Published in the United States of America

# Chapter One

It had been a long day and he needed to unwind. He left the arena and head to a local bar. A good beer with a shot of ol' Jack Daniels sounded really good at the moment. He rode on Harley, the wind blowing through his hair. There was nothing quite like sitting on his bike breezing down the highway, soaring like a bird above the ground. He could've traveled all night, and would after he stopped for just one drink.

He walked into the smoke-filled place, looked around at the clientele, and went over to the bar and ordered a drink. As he leaned on the bar waiting, he noticed in a corner of the room a couple of guys were arm wrestling. In the next room were pool tables, and there seemed to be a tournament going. The bar was noisy with music playing and a few couples were dancing. Everyone seemed to be enjoying themselves.

His thoughts were interrupted by the bartender handing him his drink. He paid and gave him a nice tip, then took a seat at one of the tables. Finally, he could relax. His body was aching from the night's events. He took a couple of swigs of the drink as he continued to scan the place.

That's when he noticed her standing close to the bar, watching him. He returned the stare, assessing her body. She saw that he was giving her the once over and decided to go join him. She had spotted him as he entered and thought he was a good-sized man and very handsome. She was turned on from the moment she saw him, and she could tell he wasn't from these parts. She sauntered over and stopped just inches from his table.

He looked her over much more meticulously this time, without saying a word. He thought she was attractive, but with a little too much make-up. He figured her to be about five-nine. She was very slender and had long blonde hair that hung loosely over her shoulders. She was a little pale for the ruby red lips. Her eye shadow was right out of Elvira's make-up case, which distracted one from her bluish-green eyes. She was dressed in a white halter top, black leather skirt and jacket. She wore fish-net stockings and spiked black heels.

She remained standing until he offered her a seat. He tilted his head toward the chair, and gave it a gentle shove with his foot. She sat down, never taking her eyes off him. She liked what she saw before her and thought about what a fine specimen of man he was.

She figured he stood about seven feet tall. His hair was combed back into a braid with a bandanna wrapped around his head. He wore all black; shirt, jeans and boots, and a long leather jacket that stopped at his ankles. But what struck her the most was his clear, green, seductive, eyes.

She wanted him badly, and wasn't afraid to let him know it. He was watching her admiring him, and knew what she wanted. It was always this way. Because of his size, they felt every part of him would be proportionately pleasing. They lusted after him expecting he could fulfill their needs in bed. And though that would ring true, it wasn't the same for him. He would leave them basking in their afterglow, while he walked away as empty as he had arrived.

"Hello, stranger, my name is Ruby," she introduced herself.

"Hi there," he replied.

"Come with me and I can make your fantasies come true," she said in a low sensual voice, wasting no time.

She rose from her seat and leaned over. She gently brushed his lips with her tongue and beckoned for him to follow her. He finished the last of his drink and followed her, observing the way she moved her hips.

She took him to her room over the bar. It wasn't very big, but it was clean. She wasted no time before removing his clothes. She kissed him on various parts of his body, arousing him even more. She removed her clothing and went to the bed. She patted the place next to her. He slowly walked over to the bed and stood before her. She looked at him, approving of his assets, then reached out to caress him. At that moment, his thoughts left the room and began to think about someone else; a fantasy woman who would routinely enter his thoughts. She was so beautiful.

He thought of her silky, soft, brown skin under his touch. How she gently ran her hands over his body. Her feathery lips as they explored him to find the spot that would send his emotions soaring. He recalled how her mouth latched hungrily on to his, making him quiver with desire.

He came out of his thoughts and found himself lying next to the woman he'd just met. She laid breathing hard. If she did any harder, she would be snoring. He looked at her closely as she slept without all her make-up. She didn't look all that good after all, he thought to himself.

It had been a night like so many others. He would constantly have to go to his dream woman to get through the deed. He left her bed and went to shower. They had done all there was to be done. After dressing he walked over to her as she had woken, and gave her a long look. Then he left a bill on the nightstand by her bed. He turned away and went through the door without a word. She sat up in the bed and took the bill in her hands, giving it a sniff and kiss. Not bad for thirty minutes with the big guy, she thought.

She heard him start up his bike and ride away. "Good, she said to herself. "He's gone." She showered and got ready to pick up her next trick. When she had just finished dressing, she heard the motorcycle coming back. "He must be coming back for more of me," she said. "Maybe I won't have to go out after all."

There was a knock at her door, and she quickly let the man in. He immediately took her into his arms, kissing her roughly while guiding her to the bed. They laid down, still locked in a kiss, and she moved her hands over his body. He unlocked their lips and stared down into her eyes. At that moment, she had a harsh realization and opened her mouth to scream, but he quickly placed a hand at her throat. There would be no more tricks this night or any other night.

The man walked out of her room and rode away. He left a note on the nightstand next to the money: "Never make promises you can't keep."

# Chapter Two

Brenna rushed into the office carrying her purse, arms full of paperwork, and a doughnut in her mouth with a cup of coffee in one hand. The phone was ringing and she ran to catch it before it stopped. She dropped her things onto the desk and snatched the receiver from the cradle.

"Hello," she called into it, nearly out of breath.

But she was too late. They'd hung up. She slammed the receiver back down, walked behind her desk and sat down in her chair. Then she picked up the doughnut and took a nice chunk out of it, followed by her French-vanilla coffee. She picked up her tablet and discovered a news article about a young woman who'd been strangled to death, but she was interrupted by a knock at the door.

"Come in. The door isn't locked."

She didn't raise her head when the visitor entered. "What can I do for you?" she asked.

"Well, you can start by having dinner with me tonight," the person replied.

Brenna looked up and was surprised to see the handsome man who stood there. Skin like glistening chocolate, a tailored suit that just fit his chiseled physique, and that ever-charming smile. As always, he was a welcome sight.

"Grant, what are you doing here?" she asked excitedly, leaving her chair to jump into his arms.

He planted a wet one on her lips and she thought of a better question. "How long are you going to be in town?" she asked, sliding slowly down his front and arousing him immediately. He chuckled and she was pleased.

Brenna had gone to school with Grant Mitchum in Phoenix, Arizona. They'd been lovers up until a year ago when she'd left for New York. They'd parted on good terms, but every now and then he would try to convince her to come back to him. His feelings for her were stronger than her feelings were for him. It was one of the reasons she'd left. He was getting too serious. She cared about him, but always felt there was something missing in their relationship. She knew that what she wanted he could never give her. They were much better as friends.

"I'm here for a day or so," said Grant. "I came in yesterday to take care of some business." He missed her bad. Her athletic body, smooth brown skin and deep brown eyes pulled him right in. "I know just the place we can go," he said. "It's a nightclub and restaurant. It's the one that Wreaking Havoc Wrestling opened up here in New York. There's a show tonight; we could go to both."

"I could never understand the thrill of seeing men throwing each other around," she said.

"A friend of mine happens to be a wrestler," he revealed. "We met a couple of years ago. We're both from Sun Valley and we hit it off. He's in town tonight and gave me tickets. Go with me to the show, then afterwards we'll go to the club."

She thought about it for a moment, then agreed. It was something they hadn't done together before and she thought it might be fun.

When Grant left, she returned to the article. The murdered woman was a prostitute and killed in her own apartment. Brenna hated things like this. No one deserves to have their life taken away. She began to remember why she'd left the force. It hadn't been all about Grant, though a lot of it was him. She had come upon the body of a young woman who had been struck on the head and then strangled. Her neck was so traumatized. The man who had done it had to have been a man of enormous size. It had been more than she could take. She never wanted to see anything like that again. She continued to read until she sensed something familiar about the case.

## Chapter Three

It had been a long and grueling day with autograph
sessions, and meetings with the brass. All he wanted was
for this to be over. He sat in his dressing room hoping for
some solitude before the show. A knock at the door
interrupted that.

"What?" he snapped.

"Uh, someone to see you, sir," said a shaky voice.

He went to the door and swung it open. He was
about to send whoever it was packing. It had been a young
attendant, who'd fled at the turn of the knob, and Grant
Mitchum, who was left standing.

"Grant, you came after all," said the man. "It's good
to see a friendly face again. Come on in."

"Hey, Malcolm," said Grant. "How've you been?" he
asked his friend, giving him a quick hug.

"I've been okay," said Malcolm. "But you know how it gets when you feel like you're in a rut."

Grant sensed Malcolm needed a few words of encouragement. "A rut? Man, you're known all over the world and you've got chicks running after you all the time. What I wouldn't give to be in the rut you're in."

"If I had the power," said Malcolm, "I would grant you that wish. It's not all that it seems" he drifted off, thinking about how he would change things if he could.

"Sure," said Grant. "Are you going to tell me you can't get laid anytime you want?"

"Yes, I can," said Malcolm. "Anytime. Anywhere. Anyone. That gets old. I wish I had one special person to come home to after a hard road trip. Just to know that when we make love, we're making love. Not that empty stuff that leaves you feeling cold and degraded." He started to get angry thinking about it."

"You sure have the blues," said Grant. Then he worried if seeing him and Brenna together would be like salt in the wound, even though they weren't an item. "Hey, I'm planning to bring my ex-girlfriend with me tonight. You okay with that?"

"Sure. As long as she doesn't do that 'I watch you on TV all the time' bit." He had no problem with his true fans. They had a lot of respect for him. It was the ones who wanted to play games that bothered him. He never considered them to be real fans.

"Don't worry," said Grant with a smile. "I'll keep her in line. She'll pretend she doesn't even know who you are."

"Good," said Malcolm.

The men said their goodbyes and Malcolm closed the door and went back to his mood.

Brenna had been thinking about the murdered woman in Pittsburgh. Why did this story have a lingering impression on her? She looked at her watch. It was later than she thought. Grant would be at her apartment soon. She locked up and hurried home. As soon as she got home, she started removing her clothing and headed for the shower. In her haste, she'd forgotten to lock the front door.

Once in the shower, she was thinking about Grant. Because of the running water, and her distracted thoughts, she didn't hear the door being opened to her apartment. When she was done, she dried off and went to the bedroom. She threw the towel on the bed and proceeded to search for something to wear. Should she go casual? No. She's always wearing casual. How about conservative? No. This was a wrestling show, and a nightclub afterwards. And anyway, she wanted to look good for Grant. Just because they weren't together didn't mean they couldn't have a little wrestling match of their own later on. Maybe sexy. She laughed at that. No one would mistake her for sexy.

She elected for a mixture. She chose a white button-down blouse and decided she would leave the first few buttons undone, to show some cleavage. Next was a pair of beige jeans that clung to her figure, low-cut leather boots and a leather jacket. Still in the nude, she looked in the mirror and thought about what to do with her hair. It was very short, highlighted, and curly. She laughed to herself. Comb it, is all she had to do.

"It's been a long time since I've seen that view," said a voice. "And it's a nice one at that."

Brenna quickly reached for the towel to cover herself. Grant was standing in the doorway, leaning against the frame.

"Grant, you scared me!" shouted Brenna. "How did you get in here?" She sat on her bed and let out a long breath, relieved that it wasn't someone else.

"Do you always keep your door unlocked, inviting who knows what?" he asked.

Seeing that she was shaken up, he sat down next to her and put his arm around her. She calmed down and bit and began to respond to his touch. He was already aroused by her nakedness. She didn't know he'd seen her come out of the bathroom and had been watching her, thinking of how good their love making had always been. He'd averted his eyes several times, telling himself they're only friends.

It had been a long time since she'd had anyone in her bed. She didn't want to lead him on, but she uncontrollably reached out and touched his chest. She could feel his hair through the shirt. It felt good to touch a man. He groaned at her touch. Soft as always.

He took the towel and threw it behind them, and laid her back onto the bed. She looked into his brown eyes, as he lowered his mouth to hers, gently flicking her lips with his tongue. She opened her mouth invitingly. He began to caress her breast causing her to moan. She began to unbutton his shirt. He didn't let her finish before he ripped the buttons loose, throwing the shirt off, and stood up and took off the rest of his clothing. She smiled at his enthusiasm. She scooted back on the bed, giving him the once over. She always admired his six-foot-nine frame and all the other qualities that came along with it.

He looked at her knowingly. Crawling over her, he gently lowered his body to hers and they held each other tight and kissed deeply. As far as he was concerned, they had a lot of time to make up for, and little time to do it. They gently explored each other's bodies, savoring each touch.

He gave her everything he had and she happily welcomed it. When they were both were expended, they drifted off to sleep.

# Chapter Four

Malcolm thought of his visit with Grant and started to think about their childhood. They'd been the best of friends when they were young, even got into trouble together as children often do. He thought about how much easier life was then, and how Grant and his family moved away. They'd lost touch until seeing each other at a wrestling match a couple of years prior. Grant was in the audience with friends. He'd told them he was friends with the Grim Reaper, but they just laughed. Malcolm recalled that Grant had given a note to security and asked them to give it Malcolm. He'd later told Malcolm that his friends were worried they'd gotten into some kind of trouble when security hauled them to a private room. When Malcolm showed up and embraced Grant, the friends were pretty surprised, and even more-so when the two spoke of how much they missed each other and then forgot about the others in the room.

They went out after the show and had kept in touch ever since. Grant was a true friend. Malcolm had only one other friend that compared, and that was fellow wrestler Lance Connors.

Brenna jumped up and looked at the time. "Grant wake up! Look what time it is." She ran to the bathroom to take another quick shower and Grant followed.

He was immediately aroused with her so near, but she shook her head no. He had brought his suitcase with him. He would be leaving that night and had checked out of his hotel hoping he could spend it with Brenna.

As they sat in their seats, Grant tried to explain some of the storylines and describe the wrestlers, but he purposely omitted talk about Malcolm, remembering the promise he'd made his friend.

From the front row, Brenna admired the huge crowd and how pumped up they were. She read some of the signs and blushed at a few. It was a freeing feeling, being there with all the excitement, even if you weren't an established fan. Several matches took place. Just as she thought, they did throw each other around a lot, but it was more impressive than she'd imagined. These were not just high-adrenaline performers, but tremendous athletes. Athletes who could really work up a crowd.

At one point, the lights went dim, and the crowd became quieter than they had all night. They were anticipating something. Then a very large man appeared and the crowd became wild. He wore a mask, but he was well-built and at least as tall as Grant. He faced two men in what Grant explained was a handicapped match, and he won.

During that match, Grant had slipped away for a drink. He hadn't made it back yet, when the lights faded once more. This time there was total darkness. And this time, when the man appeared, the crowd really broke loose.

As he came to the ring, and the lights came back on, the man looked at Brenna and the empty seat next to her. Those were the seats he'd gifted his friend Grant. He gathered the woman was his ex. He stared at her and she stared back. She rather liked his long, wet hair and dark, come-hither stare. His vanilla skin was lightly tanned and tattoos covered his arms. He came close enough that Brenna noticed his green eyes, a shade she'd never seen before. When he turned from her and entered the ring, he told himself he would have a talk with Grant about not mentioning how lovely this woman was.

# Chapter Five

Grant and Brenna made it to the Wreaking Havoc Night Club, opened by and named for the wrestling promotion Grant's friend worked for. There were crowds of people standing on the outside to see their favorite wrestlers. As the couple entered, they were escorted to a table reserved by Malcolm.

"This place is jammin'," said Grant as he looked around at the place.

There were many wrestlers seated in their area, and many others who went out to mingle with fans and other guests.

"Yes, it is," said Brenna, trying to talk over the music.

While they waited for Malcolm, a fan asked Grant to dance, thinking he was a wrestling star. He didn't correct the young woman and went with her, flashing Brenna a shameful smile. She laughed to herself. She enjoyed watching him dance and just shook her head. He was such a clown.

"Hello. Is this seat taken?" said a deep voice.

Brenna looked up into a pair of familiar green eyes. He looked different outside the arena. He was even bigger, and very attractive. "No," said Brenna. "This seat is not taken. My friend and I are waiting for another friend of his to arrive. Please have a seat."

At that time, Grant was making his way to the table. He'd seen Malcolm come in and was giving him time to meet Brenna before he came back to the table.

"Hey, Malcolm. Did you meet Brenna?" He asked as he sat down and put his arm around her.

Malcolm continued to stare at Brenna. "We were just about to get acquainted before you arrived," he said.

"Oh, so you're the wrestling friend?" Brenna said with surprise.

"And you must be the ex," Malcolm replied.

Brenna looked at Grant with narrowed eyes for the way Malcolm had called her 'the ex', knowing Grant must have referred to her as such.

"Let's start again," Malcolm said politely. "I'm Malcolm Burkhardt."

"And I'm Brenna Sims. It's a pleasure to meet you, Malcolm Burkhardt."

He smiled when she'd repeated his name. Their eyes were fixed on each other's until Grant interrupted.

"So, Brenna. Would you like Malcolm to give you an autograph? Or would you like him to tell you something about himself?" Grant was getting ready to have his fun with Malcolm's ego.

Malcolm sat back in his chair with a frustrated look on his face. Here we go again, he thought, with the autographs and questions. Sometimes he wished they would just accept him as Malcolm. He was reaching inside his pocket for a pen when Brenna interrupted.

"Grant, how rude. Malcolm is here to unwind. He doesn't want to talk about wrestling or give out autographs. Right Malcolm?" She looked at him nodding her head.

Malcolm left the pen inside his jacket. Grant had control over this woman after all. Just as he'd promised, she was acting as if she didn't know who he was.

"Well, I don't mind," said Malcolm politely. "We're here to greet the fans and to have a good time." He wanted to make her more comfortable asking for his autograph, but she didn't, and he gave Grant an approving smile. Grant gave him a thumbs up behind her back as if to say, 'I told you I would handle her'.

"I think it's nice that you don't mind the fans," said Brenna. "I figured celebrities would always feel bothered by it when they're out in public."

Now it was coming, he thought. Now she would ask for the autograph. But still she didn't.

"You'll have to excuse me," she said. "But until tonight, I've never been to a wrestling match or seen it on TV."

Grant's cover was blown.

Malcolm leaned on the table and Grant's eyes went everywhere but to Malcolm's.

"You've never seen it until tonight? So, you don't know who I am, other than Grant's friend?"

She looked at him strangely. "Just that I saw you in the show tonight, but I never heard of you before that. Is that so strange?" What an ego, she thought to herself.

"No, no. I didn't mean it that way. It's just I was given the impression you were a huge fan." Malcolm then sat back in his chair.

Brenna was puzzled, but not for long. "I see you have been played hard, Malcolm. And when you get ready to get him back. Call me." They all had a good laugh.

Later in the evening, Grant and Brenna got up to slow dance. Malcolm watched from the table. He had enjoyed himself. Brenna was very nice; a real lady. He wondered how Grant let her get away from him. He felt he wouldn't mind getting to know her himself, but wasn't sure how 'ex' she was. Judging by the way they looked at each other, things might not be quite finished between them.

Before parting that night, Grant told Malcolm to remember that he and any of his friends were welcome to stay at his place whenever the road brought them to Phoenix.

"I'm glad to have met you," said Brenna sincerely.

"The pleasure was mine, little lady," he replied in a southern drawl.

Why hadn't she noticed that hint of an accent before? It was another plus for him, she thought. She was snapped out of her thoughts when he took her hand and kissed it. No, make that a double plus for him.

Malcolm watched Grant walk away with someone he already wished he had. He decided to have one more drink before leaving and sat back down. Then a woman sat down at his table. He knew this type of fan. This type wanted to know how good he was in bed.

"My name is Wendi," she said. "I see you've been left alone. So, have I. Why don't we go somewhere quiet? I can make it worth your while, after a hard night's work." She leaned over the table spilling even more cleavage over her tight red dress. She had a nice tan, he thought, and again, way too much makeup.

He looked her up and down and then took her to his motorcycle. He couldn't get Brenna out of his head. Grant was lucky. From the way they looked at each other when they were leaving, he knew where they were headed. He wished he could trade places.

Grant laid in Brenna's arms. He didn't want to leave her. "Come with me Brenna. Everyone you know is back home. We are great together. Can't you see that?"

"Grant, why do we have this conversation every time we talk. Sex has never been the problem, or our friendship. It's me. I need something different."

She sat up. This was as good of a time as it ever would be. "Grant though I love you. I'm not in love with you. I've tried to let you know in the nicest way as I could. You are the sweetest guy I know and you deserve better. Out there is a nice woman who will give you everything you want. It's just not me." She wrapped her robe around her and went to the window. Grant didn't say anything. He just went to shower before leaving.

Malcolm was showering as well. He asked himself why he kept spending nights like this. But what else could he do? he wondered. Become celibate? No way. If it didn't do anything else, it did give him release until the next time.

Before leaving, he'd laid a bill on the night stand. Wendi took the bill and smiled as she heard him leave on his bike. She then took a shower and returned to the bed. But she heard the motorcycle returning. He must have been impressed. Maybe it wouldn't end like the others in her life. Maybe she had found someone nice. She ran to the door at the knock. She opened it and let him in.

She was immediately engulfed in a kiss and moved forcibly to the bed. She looked at his eyes and started to holler. The scream was cut off with one hand over her mouth and the other tightening around her throat. She was right. It wouldn't end like the others.

As she lay dead, waiting to be found, there was a note on the night stand. It read: Never make promises you can't keep.

# Chapter Six

Brenna laid in bed listening to the neighbors getting ready for the day. She had decided to stay in considering the long night before. She went to get a cup of coffee and read the news.

She liked to be reminded of how the world around her was doing. She was scanning a local news site on her tablet when she came across a startling article. Another woman was strangled to death; this time right here in New York. She had an odd feeling about the article, just as she had with the other one, but she couldn't put a finger on what it was. The phone started to ring.

"Hello?"

"Hi, Brenna. I just wanted you to know that I made it home safely."

She smiled at hearing his voice. She knew he had been hurt by her words the previous night. But still, he called.

"Hi, Grant. I'm glad you made it safely. And I'm glad you aren't angry with me."

He could never be angry with her. No matter what. He knew she loved him and wanted nothing but his happiness. "When will I see you again?" he asked.

She realized they needed to redefine their relationship. "I don't know," she said. "Listen, I have to catch up on some work. Talk to you soon."

After the call, she sipped her coffee and continued to study the article. This victim was a nurse at the local hospital.

Malcolm was working out with Lance. He had been distracted all during their workout. He couldn't get Brenna out of his mind. He knew Grant had slept with her before he left, even if he did call her his 'ex'.

Still, he wished he could get to know Brenna better. But it would have to be another time. He was getting back on the road. It would probably be a month before was back in New York. In the meantime, he had to find out as much as he could about her.

"Malcolm. Where are you?" Lance asked. "You're not with it today. What's going on?"

"Nothing Lance. Just deep in my thoughts. How do you find out about someone?" He was staring forward, not looking at his friend.

Lance looked puzzled at this comment. "Why? Who is it you want to find something about?" Lance seemed a little nervous about the question, but Malcolm didn't notice.

"It's a woman I met last night," said Malcolm, smiling for the first time that day. "I'd like to get to know her better."

"You have got to be kidding me," said Lance. "You sleep with some woman who only wanted sex from you in the first place, and now you want to take her home to mama?"

Malcolm looked at Lance as he spoke these words, and couldn't understand what had come over him. "Wait a minute. Where is this coming from?" Malcolm asked.

"Man, you know as well as I do how it is," Lance replied. "They come up to you and make these promises and then they don't keep them. Makes me sick." Lance had a look in his hazel eyes Malcolm had never seen before.

"Lance, you know the drill. They know what we're looking for, and we know what they're looking for. So, no one's hurt. It's a game people play. If it's that hard, man. Then you find someone special and settle down. That's the way it is." Malcolm knew what Lance was going through. He had been there many times. He was giving him the same advice he'd given himself a thousand times.

"I'll do more than that," said Lance. "If you can't do something, then don't tell me you can," he said, looking at the floor as if in his own world. He walked away angrily.

Malcolm felt for his friend. Seems he was even more down than he was about things. Then it occurred to him to hire a private investigator. He used his phone to check for local listings. He scrolled the matches until saw a name that stood out from the rest. Could it be the same? No. There had to be many with that name. Still, he smiled to himself.

# Chapter Seven

Brenna had planned on staying in, but the cases of the murdered women were weighing on her. She went to her office to go over some old files. While pouring over them, she heard the main door open. She watched from her seat, awaiting the appearance of the unexpected guest.

Malcolm had decided to go to the address found in the listing. It was worth a shot, he'd told himself. He gathered all his courage to go meet the detective, hoping it would be the woman he wanted to see. "Brenna Sims, P.I." it had said on the website. What a coincidence. And now he was at her office. He walked in and peered through an open door to see if it was true. It was. He took in a deep breath and entered, watching the expression on her face go from curious to pleased. Evidently, he'd left a lasting impression on her as well.

"Malcolm," she said, regaining her senses.

"In the flesh," he said.

She guessed that Grant had told him her profession and that he must have need of a detective. "I'm glad to see you. What can I do for you?" she asked.

"I need you to find someone for me," he said.

"Oh, really? Who?" she asked, pulling out her notepad and beckoning him to have a seat.

Malcolm had to think fast. He couldn't very well say, "I need a detective to find you". Then he thought of someone. The girl he met the night before. He had two faults. One is, he never read the news. And two, he never followed up on the women he slept with.

"There was this girl I met last night. We spoke briefly. She did give me her name. Wendi. She stood about five-foot-seven, long black hair, had a tan, blue eyes—no, gray eyes, I think."

"She sounds like a looker," said Brenna with a grin. "How did you manage to let her leave without getting a phone number?"

In reality, she was wondering how the woman could have left Malcolm without giving her phone number. She would have in a heartbeat.

Malcolm noticed how she stared at him and began to get caught up in the moment as each began to dwell on the person sitting across from them and forget the subject at hand. But Brenna broke the spell.

"So, Malcolm," she said, refocusing her thoughts. "You don't have anything else I could go on? Like her profession, hobbies, likes or dislikes. You did have a conversation with her, right?" He has the most gorgeous eyes, she thought to herself.

"Oh, yes. We talked for a while before I left." Malcolm thought how he would love to rub his hands over Brenna's creamy dark skin.

"Is there anything else you can tell me?" she asked. She thought how she would love to be held in his powerful arms.

"That's all I can think of right now. But I have your office number. I can call you from time to time. It's hard to catch me. Unless you want my cell number?" He thought about the things he could do to her body.

"That would be great," said Brenna. "And just to be on the safe side. I'll give you mine as well." She thought how she would love to climb his trunk. She always had a passion for big men. She handed him her information and he in return.

Malcolm felt it was time for him to go. He needed a cold shower and wished she could see how she had aroused him. Brenna was glad he was leaving. She needed to go home immediately and cool off herself. He had truly aroused some feelings in her. And she had never felt this way with Grant.

Brenna walked him to the door and told him she would do her best to find the woman. They took each other's hands and stared into each other's eyes. A force was drawing them together uncontrollably. Their bodies touched; their lips neared. And then they found themselves in an embrace. He lifted her off the floor as he allowed his tongue to taste every inch of her mouth. He didn't ever want to stop, even for breath. She was his breath.

Brenna was overwhelmed by this man's fire. She could do nothing but hold on and let him unleash himself. Malcolm finally needing air, unlocked his mouth from hers. Still holding her, both breathing heavily, he looked upon her face, memorizing everything about it, so that on those lonely nights his dream lady would have a face.

Malcolm set her down gently, never taking his eyes off her. After several moments, he turned and left. He knew they would see each other again. He would make sure of it.

Brenna was still leaning against the door. Trying to catch her breath and get the strength back into her legs. "Like I said, how could she let him get away without giving her phone number?"

When she was able, with the help of the desk to lean on, she made it to her chair. She looked over the notepad and put it in her desk. She had to get home and douse this heat she felt running through her body. She could start the search tomorrow.

Driving to her apartment, Brenna never noticed that someone was following her.

# Chapter Eight

Wreaking Havoc Wrestling had gone to New Orleans and it was time for Mardi Gras. The town was alive with parades, carnivals, and dancing in the streets.

Malcolm had decided to go out and Lance tagged along. They didn't mind mingling with the crowd. With so much going on, they were just two more tourists in the crowd. They came upon a little café and ordered something to eat.

As the two men discussed the nights matches, a young woman sat in the corner watching the two giants. She was fascinated by their size and masculinity. She'd never seen any men like them before. She wore a low-cut purple sweater that hung off each shoulder, showed a lot of cleavage, and accentuated her very large breasts. Her waist was very small, and made her curvy hips look larger than they were. Her make-up was heavy for a reason.

Her eyes were such a pale blue they were almost white. She was Creole. Her family had lived in New Orleans for generations. She had a mind of her own and was an outcast in her family because of the lifestyle she chose to live.

Before the night was over, she would wish she had taken a little time to grow more. As she watched them, Malcolm feeling her stare, turned to look in her direction. Lance turned to see what he was looking at, and Malcolm felt him become irritated for some reason. He told Lance to go ahead and he would pay for the food. He gave the waiter a note to give to the young woman and left. The note said for her to meet him back there tonight.

When Brenna got home after Malcolm's visit, she couldn't get him off her mind. As she curled up on the bed, she kept replaying the office scene over and over and felt herself becoming aroused again. His scent was still on her. She happily fell to sleep dreaming of him.

Sometime later, she was awoken by her cell phone ringing. She reached for it and almost knocked it to the floor. "Hello," she said, still waking up.

"Did I wake you?" said Malcolm. "I didn't know you would be sleeping so early."

At the sound of his voice, she had woken completely and sat up straight away. "No, it's okay. I was just sitting here and dozed off."

"I just remembered something about the woman I asked you to find," Malcolm said. "I think she was a nurse."

Malcolm couldn't see the hurt on Brenna's face upon him mentioning this other woman.

"That would be helpful." She strained to say this, not wanting him to know what she was feeling.

"I'm going to get started on it first thing in the morning, and I'll give you a call as soon as I find something out. Talk to you later." She hung the phone up and began to wonder how she could have thought that he would've wanted her.

Malcolm stared at the phone for a while, wondering why she had hung up so abruptly. He had wanted to talk more. He thought with what had happened in her office she would be more receptive with him. Then he realized. "What an idiot." She did feel something, and what did he do? He called her about finding some other woman. He was calling her back when Lance appeared.

"Malcolm, what's up with you?" Lance asked with annoyance in his voice.

"What's going on with you, man?" Malcolm put down the phone. He turned toward Lance, getting a little irritated at his mood of late.

"I asked you first," said Lance.

"Look, I don't have time for your moods or your games." Malcolm began to walk away, still a little angry with himself for being so thoughtless with Brenna. He was going to have to make this up to her.

"No. You don't have time for important things but you always have time for your, what are they called, oh yeah, whores?" He was trying to anger Malcolm for some reason.

Malcolm ignored him and walked away. Play the games all you want, Malcolm thought. I can play too.

## Chapter Nine

Malcolm had met up with the young woman after the show and went to her apartment. She had enjoyed the ride on his bike. Malcolm couldn't figure it out, but something about her struck him as odd. He would soon find out. When she got close, he could see that she had on even more make-up then the other women he had bedded.

He asked her to remove it, and was shocked to see that she was so young. To his eyes, she was just a child. He grew very angry and told her so. He put some money on the table and told her to go home to her family. Then he left. She picked up the money and laughed as she heard his bike roar off. She enjoyed playing with men. She felt they were all stupid. No one could tell at first how young she was. And no one knew that she was a virgin. She liked to tease men, and so far, they had always run off, but not before she'd got money from them or stolen their wallet.

She stood still as she heard the sound of the bike returning. What could he want? He left out of here angry enough to kill her. She wasn't sure she wanted to let him in when he knocked. Hesitantly, she opened the door.

She was immediately attacked. She tried to push her assailant away, but he was too powerful. She struggled against him as he laid her on the bed and pressed into her. She couldn't move. She looked into his eyes and began to scream. But with all the celebrations outside, no one could hear her.

He tore her clothes from her body with one hand and held her down while she kicked and clawed. It was useless. Moments later, her screaming had stopped. She laid there staring in shock. He looked at her as he straightened his clothes. Then he left his signature note by the bed. Traumatized, she never heard him ride away.

The next day, Brenna read about the most recent attack. A young woman had been brutally raped and beaten. The girl was alive but disoriented and confused, and doctors had no idea of how soon she would come out of it.

The news stated that the young woman was the granddaughter of a well-known businessman and that evidence at the scene suggested the attacker was the same person who'd committed the recent murders in Pittsburgh and New York. Police hadn't disclosed what this evidence was. Brenna decided to review the article about the New York murder. It read:

Local nurse killed in her apartment. Wendi Vasquez, was found murdered in her apartment after not showing up to work. Friends and family worried, went to check on her and found her strangled body.

Brenna re-read the description of the woman and pulled out her notepad. Her mouth fell opened as realized the description of the dead woman matched the nurse Malcolm was trying to locate. It couldn't be the same woman—could it? Well, Malcolm wasn't involved, she rationalized, he said he hadn't left with her. So that was that.

She had to make a phone call. She needed more information on this case. There was still something nagging her about these cases that she couldn't figure out.

"Hi, Rico. How has life been treating you?" she said in her sexiest voice.

"You are a tease. Have I ever told you that?" he asked.

"All the time. Why don't we have lunch together? It's been a while," she said, flicking her pencil.

"Okay. Let's not play the game. There's something you want."

Rico, a police detective, was onto her as usual. "Rico, I'm deeply hurt. Even if I did want some info, I would still want to see you, for old time's sake."

They had met during one of her investigations and had almost become lovers. But she found out he was married. After some time however, they'd agreed to remain close friends.

"Okay. How about our favorite lunch bar?" He wanted to remind her of what they could have had, but he didn't. She didn't know he'd had fallen in love with her back then and was ready to tell his wife he wanted a divorce. They'd been separated for a while, but before he told Brenna the truth, a friend of his made the reveal for him. The rest was history.

Brenna met Rico at the lunch bar and she asked him about the three cases. She also mentioned Malcolm's nurse friend.

"You think there may be a connection, between your friend's lady and the one found dead?" he asked.

"You haven't been able to find the killer because there hasn't been anything you could connected them with," she explained.

He leaned forward on the table. "Them? What do you mean by them?" he asked.

"You're not treating this case as serial killings?" She was surprised, but maybe the undisclosed evidence didn't match.

"No. We don't have enough to prove it's the work of one person. And if it is, the killer sure does a lot of traveling. The crimes are in different states."

He shook his head and rubbed his eyes.

"Why so tired?" she asked.

He averted his eyes almost bashfully and she was on to him.

"Too much of a good thing?" she laughed.

"That is none of your business," he said with a grin. He still cared about her, but he respected her decision. Besides, he wasn't about to mess up a good thing with his new lady love. He'd waited too long for someone like her to come into his life.

"I'm glad you are happy," said Brenna.

He knew she meant it. He hoped someone could come into her life and make her just as happy.

"Now, I need all the information you can give me on these cases."

He could see that he wasn't going to get any rest until she got what she wanted. He told her he would get the information and call her later in the day. She was satisfied.

# Chapter Ten

Wreaking Havoc had arrived in Houston, Texas. Malcolm lived there and invited his friends and fellow performers Lance, Andy, and Brad to stay at his place. After settling in, Malcolm went out for a night on the town without the guys.

At a bar, he met a woman named June. She was about five-foot-eleven and had long, flaming red hair. He'd felt her eyes on him and turned to see her. He thought she was quite pretty.

She'd been admiring him since he'd come through the door. She wasn't sure if she should approach him. But when Malcolm turned to meet her gaze, it wasn't long before he beckoned her to join him. She was glad.

"Hello. My name is June. I watched as you came in. Do you work out?" she asked, gazing over his frame.

"Yeah. It's a job necessity," he replied. "You look like you work out yourself."

"Yes. I'm not into the bulging muscles as much as fitness. It came with me being so tall. What kind of work do you do?" She figured he might be a bouncer or a bodyguard.

"You don't know me?" He was happy.

"Should I?" She looked at him a little confused.

"I wrestle for a living. I'm the Grim Reaper. Malcolm is my real name." He watched and she didn't seem overly enthused. Somehow, this pleased him even more.

"Oh yeah, I've heard of you. My brothers watch wrestling. I don't have much time to watch TV."

Normally she didn't pick up strangers, but something about him was striking. Very seldom has she found men who towered over her. She was going to enjoy being engulfed in a man's arms.

As if reading her thoughts, Malcolm asked, "Would you like to go somewhere a little quieter?"

"I have a hotel room not too far away," she replied. "Would you like to go there?" She got up from the table and he followed.

They rode on his bike and laughed and had a great time. When they got to her room, she poured him a drink. They talked for a while, but both wanted each other badly. Finally, they couldn't restrain themselves any longer. Malcolm guided her out of her chair and pressed his lips against hers. She tilted her head back invitingly. It felt good

52

to her to look up at someone larger and taller than she was. She ran her hands over his massive arms, feeling his firm muscles. She was in heaven as she glided her hands over his hard chest. She groaned as he moved his tongue over her neck and to her earlobe and then back to reclaim her mouth. He moved her to the bed, lying her gently down. But she popped back up and shoved him down on the bed instead, and began to remove his clothing.

He liked it when they took control. It was all too rare. She kissed his chest and ran her tongue over his hardened nipples as he moaned. She nibbled one and then the other, then continue downward. She slowly lowered his pants, heightening his desire. She stopped only to take in the object of her desire.

She began to caress him, then he tossed her to the bed and returned the favor of removing her clothing, as he licked and nibbled, sending her into a frenzy. They played this top and bottom game for what seemed like hours. It had been a long time since he had enjoyed someone so fully. They laid in each other's arms, until they drifted off to sleep.

Just before dawn, Malcolm took a shower and dressed. He looked down at her sleeping. He had enjoyed himself with her. He left his number by the bedside, hoping she would call him. He gently kissed her, not wanting to wake her. Then he left.

June woke to the sound of a rumbling motorcycle. She looked over to see that Malcolm was gone. She never saw the note he'd left. There was a knock at the door. Malcolm, she thought. She ran to open it. And before she could say anything, she was ambushed by an aggressive embrace and hungry kiss.

She was forced gradually to the bed and then laid down. When she looked at him, she started to scream, but a hand went quickly over her mouth, another to her throat. As her aggressor tightened his grip, she kicked him hard between the legs. He fell off of her in pain.

She gasped for breath and tried to roll off the bed. He grabbed her leg, and she fell to the floor. She gave him a hard kick to the face, making him loosen his grip. She kicked him again harder and he finally let go.

She scrambled for the door and tried to get to her feet before she felt him grab her from behind by the hair. He gave her a hard fist to the face, sending her back to the bed as he followed, even angrier than before. He pounced on her and began to hit her with his fist over and over until she succumbed to the darkness.

Malcolm arrived home in the early morning and slipped in unnoticed, or so he'd thought. When he joined the other guys for breakfast, he was met with some sly looks.

"So, how was your night?" Andy asked.

"It was okay. And yours?"

"Oh, fine," said Andy with a crooked smile.

"Say, where's Lance? Sleeping in today?"

"No," said Brad. "He said he was going to look for you last night."

"I haven't seen him," said Malcolm, wondering why Lance hadn't called his cell phone if he'd been wondering where he was. Then again, Lance had been behaving strangely as of late.

While talking, they heard Lance come in. He went straight upstairs without saying anything to anyone. There were a number of raised brows.

Lance stayed in his room all day. Later, when he thought everyone had left, he went down to get something to eat. He was surprised by someone sitting at the table.

"Damn! What happened to your face?" Brad asked.

Malcolm decided he didn't want to wait and see if June would call him. He went to her hotel room. She didn't answer. Then one of the housekeepers saw him at the door and explained she'd been taken to the hospital. Someone had beaten her badly. They didn't know if she was going to make it.

Malcolm learned from the manager what hospital she'd been taken too, but once he arrived, he was told she was in critical condition and was heavily guarded. He couldn't understand who could do something like this. As he was turning to leave, he was stopped by police.

"Malcolm Burkhardt?"

"Yes."

"We need you to come down to the station with us."

Malcolm was stunned. Surely, they didn't suspect him of this horrible crime. He looked over his shoulder at June's room and then followed the officers peacefully.

# Chapter Eleven

Sharon Jones was in Phoenix on business. A guest was supposed to join her in few days, but he'd already cancelled. That wouldn't put a damper on her plans, however. She'd come to realize that he didn't love her in the same way that she loved him. He'd disappointed her one time too many. So, she decided that when her business was complete, she would stay and vacation as long as she liked. For once, she was going to do something for Sharon. She would relax and enjoy herself, and heal.

While perusing the local art section of an antique shop, she accidentally bumped into a man of immense size. "My apologies," she said quickly. When she looked up, he was all chest. And a nice chest at that, she thought. When their eyes met, her breath was taken away. "Oh," she muttered. He was very handsome.

Grant stared down at the lovely lady with a smile, and she suddenly realized she was gawking at the man. She turned away in realization and he smiled even more.

"Please excuse me," said Sharon, returning her gaze to the carvings and sketches.

"No, excuse me," Grant said kindly. "Are you from around here?" he asked, simply trying to make conversation, whether she was from there or not. For a second, her mannerisms, her skin, her smile, reminded him of Brenna. But she had a unique beauty that was all her own.

"No, I'm from L.A.," she replied. "I'm on an overdue vacation."

"I don't want to seem forward," said Grant, "but I can show you around a bit, if you'd like." He gave her one of his charming smiles and clasped his hands as if pleading. How could she resist?

She thought hard for a moment. He seemed like a nice guy. "All right. Where to first?" she asked.

"How about lunch?"

She agreed with a smile. Grant was looking forward to this very much. He was quite taken with this woman already.

Rico walked into Brenna's office with a folder in his hand. "This is confidential," he said sternly. "I don't know what you're going to do with the information. But don't do anything that might put you in danger."

"Why, Rico, I didn't know that you cared," Brenna said.

She was taking his words lightly, but he was very concerned. "Seriously, Brenna. You know how you are. Remember how we met?"

Just after she'd moved to New York, Brenna used herself as a decoy to catch a longtime suspect and had nearly been raped. Rico was off-duty and sensed that something was wrong when he saw a man following her. So, Rico secretly followed them both. He saw the man come up behind her and Rico knocked him out with his gun.

"I'll be careful," Brenna promised. "I won't do anything that will put my life in danger. I'm just trying to put some pieces together. There's something about this case that's so familiar. I can't my finger on it. But it's there. If only I could figure it out."

Rico shook his head as he watched her go over the contents of the folder. He told himself, once a police detective, always a police detective. She never noticed him leave.

Brenna pondered the fact that a note had been left at each crime scene, and that the crimes were in different cities. She had to consider that the suspect was a regular traveler. Having learned there were similar attacks in New Orleans and Houston, although both victims had lived, she believed they were related and decided to follow the suspect's footsteps.

She started making flight reservations right away. And when she called Rico to tell him she was heading to New Orleans, he wanted to know why.

"It's Mardi Gras," she answered. She didn't know if he was convinced.

"Okay, Bren. Just be careful. Promise me you will at least do that." He knew the truth. He'd just got news of the brutal attack down there.

"I promise," said Brenna. She knew that he knew the truth. She could hear it in his voice. They said their goodbyes and she went home to prepare for the last-minute flight.


The police released Malcolm. They seemed satisfied with his answers. Their knowing who he was didn't hurt much, either. They even asked for a few autographs for their kids. He obliged. He just wanted to get out of there as quickly and as amicably as possible. When he arrived at the ranch, the other men were glad to see him. They'd been worried about where he'd disappeared to.

"Man, none of you will believe this," he said. "I was with this chick last night, and today she's unconscious in the hospital. Someone beat her. Bad. They thought it was me. She can't tell them until she wakes up, but I think they're finally convinced it wasn't me."

Just as he finished explaining, Lance walked in. "Where have you been, Malcolm? Out with another one of your sluts?"

Malcolm was getting an eerie feeling about all of this. "Where were you, Lance? And what the hell happened to your face?"

Lance never answered, leaving the other men to stare at him, confused.

# Chapter Twelve

After checking into a hotel in New Orleans, the first thing Brenna did was notify the local police that she was on an official investigation. Then she went to the last place the victim was seen before the attack. A witness gave her a description of the man she'd left with. Then she visited the victim's apartment. She was told by neighbors that the girl had an argument with the man she'd arrived with and that he'd left on a motorcycle, only to return a few minutes later.

She didn't want to go to the family. They'd been through enough. The girl was reportedly institutionalized. She would be no help at all. She headed back to her motel room to go over the data she had gathered.

The description of the man concerned her. But she couldn't jump to conclusions. She needed more information. She had to get to Houston. Maybe someone saw who this other unfortunate woman left with. An idea popped in her head. She made a phone call.

"Rico, I need a favor. Did anyone describe the man last seen with the murdered nurse? I don't see that in the file."

"What was that you said about going to Mardi Gras?" asked Rico.

"All right. You and I both know what I'm really doing," she said.

He chuckled knowingly. "I'm knee deep right now. But I'll give you a call when I get the info."

"I'll be waiting to hear from you. And Rico...."

"Yeah?"

"Thanks."

"Hey, you know I'll do anything for you."

"Yeah. That's why I said thanks."

Malcolm was really concerned about Lance. His behavior. His face. He took a swig of beer and thought hard. Unintentionally, thoughts of the crime came into his thoughts. June had been in a struggle. Lance has been acting strange and angry lately. What if he'd followed them to her place? What if he'd tried to come on to her after he'd left and then attacked her? No way. Not Lance. He wouldn't hurt a woman. Never. Besides, they said a man showed up on a bike after he'd left. Lance had never ridden a motorcycle.

He took another drink of that beer when Andy and Brad got back from training. "Guess who we just saw riding a motorcycle. Lance, of all people. And it's even bigger than yours, man."

It was late evening when Brenna arrived in Houston. She picked up a rental car and checked into a motel in the outskirts of the city. The motel clerk told her a good place to get a bite to eat, so she went to her room to freshen up before going out.

Malcolm had been disturbed since he heard the news of Lance riding the bike. Lance had always refused to ride. Had a thing about it since he was a kid. He was knocked out of his thoughts when Lance entered the room and headed to the bar for a drink.

Malcolm wouldn't wait any longer. They seriously needed to talk, once and for all. "Lance, I want you to tell me what's been eatin' you. You've had an attitude that's out of this world. You haven't been yourself. What's going on?"

Lance stared directly at Malcolm. "Look, you may play my big brother on TV, but you're not, so get off my back."

Malcolm stood and looked hard into Lance's eyes. "No, I'm not your brother, but I thought we were friends." He slammed down his own drink and left the house.

Lance threw his beer glass against the brick wall, shattering it. He stormed to the door just in time to see Malcolm on his motorcycle, speeding away. "Damn!" he yelled. "I can't let my problems interfere with my friendship with Malcolm. This has nothing to do with him. It's me. What have I done?" He decided to take the car and follow Malcolm.

# Chapter Thirteen

Brenna arrived at a roadhouse that was highly recommended by the motel clerk. She liked the festive atmosphere. She went to sit at a table and order something to eat. A few of the local boys watched her come through the door and were deciding which one would do her the honor of picking her up for the night.

She scanned the place, and in no time, she had already spotted them. Three men she counted. Friday night. Just got paid. Already too much to drink. Nice.

One mustered up the nerve to come over and plant himself in the seat in front of her.

"Well, girlie. Yer in luck. I'm gonna make yer night," he said, giving her a toothless grin.

"I'm very flattered and all, but I'm waiting for someone," she lied, looking around as if in search of somebody.

"Well, hon', I'll just keep ya' company 'til' yer guest gets here." He was an expert on brush offs and wasn't falling for her trick. "But I'm a little curious. Why would any man in his right mind let a gorgeous lil' lady like yerself sit alone in a bar waitin' for him?" He took a gulp of beer, smiling deviously.

"Maybe she knows I won't leave her waitin' for long. Hi, lil' darlin'!" Malcolm said to Brenna with a wink. Then he bent down and kissed her on the lips.

Brenna was at a loss for words as Malcolm stared into her eyes adoringly. Then straightening up his back, Malcolm turned to the man standing before him with a look of challenge. The man conceded quickly with both hands in the air and walked away. His friends just laughed at him.

Brenna was still very surprised. "Malcolm, what are you doing here?" she asked as he took the vacant seat in front of her.

"Rescuing the most beautiful woman I've ever had the pleasure to meet," he said, taking her hand into his.

Brenna looked away shyly.

He could hardly believe he would by chance meet her here. He remembered the last time they'd spoken, and that she'd abruptly hung up the phone. It made him realize she must have felt something when they kissed in her office.

He certainly had. And now that she was near, he was going to make the best of this encounter. "I live in Houston," he explained. "And I'm sure glad I happened by here. May I ask what you're doing here? It's a long way from New York."

"Well, confidentially, I'm on a case. And I'm sorry, I can't tell you more."

She was enjoying having him near. She could still feel his mouth on her lips, and she desired more. She was hoping he wasn't there to meet somebody.

"So, Malcolm, are you waiting for someone?"

Malcolm raised an eyebrow knowingly. "The person I've been waiting for happens to be sitting right across from me," he replied. "And unless she objects, I would like to spend the rest of the night with her."

The couple was so absorbed in each other that neither noticed the pair of angry eyes watching them. When they left the roadhouse together on his motorcycle, Lance was there. He followed them in his car.

Back in New York. Rico had pulled out the information Brenna requested. It was late, he was tired. He looked over the file. Finding something interesting, he tried to call Brenna. She didn't answer, so he left her a message. He continued to read over the file and read:

"…arrived with a man on a motorcycle and went into her apartment… he was about seven feet tall. Long black leather coat. Long hair. Dark glasses. The man left half-an-hour later but returned for fifteen minutes and left again."

Then he read that the victim was last seen before that at the Wreaking Havoc Nightclub. Rico's mind went into overdrive. He decided to gather all of the data he could related to all of these recent crimes so he could review them simultaneously. Maybe Brenna was right. Maybe they were connected.

# Chapter Fourteen

Malcolm sped down the road, Brenna clinging tightly to him. Soon they came to a stop and dismounted. They were on a hill looking down over the city. He went to sit on a rock and she went to his side.

"I come here often when I want to get away from the noise," said Malcolm. "I have a house not far from here. I would take you there, but I have some company."

Brenna took the comment wrongly. When he said 'company', she assumed it meant a woman. She noticeably stiffened and Malcolm pulled her closer.

"I don't want to share you tonight with my wrestling buddies," he explained. "If I should take you there, they'll never leave us alone. Out here we will be."

Brenna was relieved. She smiled happily and sat on his lap, facing him, and wrapped her legs tightly around him. He cupped her head in his hands and pulled her in for a kiss. He delved his tongue into her mouth tasting and savoring her flavor. She moaned in desire and need for his touch, his body, all of him. She rocked slowly against him, and he nearly lost control. But he suddenly stood up and carried her to his bike.

"Not this way. Not here. Not for you," he said. Then he mounted the bike and drove them away to retrieve her car. Brenna rested her head on his back, as she gripped his waist. She didn't understand what had happened. She knew he wanted her as much as she wanted him. So why did he stop?

They got to her car and he said he would see her safely to her motel room. When they arrived there, he went in with her to make sure everything was safe. After he was satisfied, he turned to leave, but she grabbed his arm. Her eyes were so pleading, he couldn't resist her. He bent down and began kissing her harder than before.

As he held her in his arms, he rolled his tongue around in her mouth, tasting her, sucking her tongue. She couldn't help but moan. He then took her to the bed and they began to explore each other. He caressed her breasts; she massaged his hard, swollen member.

But Malcolm stopped again. He left the bed and paced the floor, running his hands through his hair. His heart was racing. His breathing was hard. He'd never felt this way for anyone, and he didn't want to share this moment in some dingy motel room. He wanted her in his house, in his room, in his bed.

Brenna looked at him confused.

"I have to leave," he said. "I'm sorry. He started for the door and then turned to gaze into her eyes. "I find you very desirable. Please understand that. I want you in the worst way. And now that I know you want me as much. I will have you, but not like this." He turned and walked out the door.

Brenna listened as the rumble of his bike fired up and then slowly faded into the distance. She couldn't believe what just happened. Twice she almost had him. And twice he'd left her wanting him. She wasn't sure what he meant, but he did say he wanted her. She would just have to be patient.

She went to take a shower before turning in when she barely saw the notification light blinking on her phone. There was a message in her business voicemail box so she called in to listen. She heard Rico's voice:

Brenna, I tried calling your cell, but didn't get an answer. Here's the info you wanted. The nurse was seen entering her apartment with a very large man. Maybe seven feet, long hair, long leather coat, sunglasses, motorcycle. I'm looking into the possible connection you mentioned and will call you with any news. Brenna, be careful. He's still out there.

Brenna was frozen still. That description fit Malcolm in every detail. She remembered what he wore that night and yes there was a long leather coat, and he had his shades with him. He said he knew the woman. But he'd lied about leaving her at the bar. He did go home with her.

Brenna swallowed hard. She could still feel his touch all over her body. Was he the killer? She started to panic. "Why else would he have lied to me?" she asked aloud. But then she heard the sound of his bike returning. Her heart nearly stopped. She waited as she heard the motorcycle engine cut off. She backed up to the far wall as she heard footsteps nearing her door. She jumped at the first sound of the pound on the door. And then the second. She slumped to the floor and didn't make a sound. Soon the pounding stopped and the footsteps slowly faded away. The bike sounded and could be heard speeding off down the road. Then there was silence.

She went to the bed and fell onto it. He'd come back to kill her. How could she be so wrong about someone? She allowed the tears to fall.

Grant and Sharon had been enjoying their continued time together. He'd proved to be everything she had thought he would be: very sweet, humorous, and always a gentleman.

Grant was smitten with her as well. He couldn't get her off his mind. He could fall in love with her. To find that once a joy, but to find it twice was glorious. He took her number out and stared at it for a moment deciding if he should call her or not. He didn't want to come off as pushy. He elected not to and decided to go to bed. He kept thinking about her however, and knowing she would go back to L.A. before long, he wanted to make the most of her time here.

# Chapter Fifteen

In the morning, Brenna was jolted out of her sleep when her alarm went off. She sat straight up in bed. She was startled awake but still groggy. When her head cleared, she remembered the night before. She pulled her pillow to her, tightening her grip. He'd come back for her as he'd done the others.

She allowed the tears to flow once more, asking herself yet again, how she could've been so wrong about him. He was so gentle with her, and loving. She couldn't believe this had happened. How could he be so passionate one moment and supposedly cruel the next? It just couldn't be.

The more she thought about it, her gut told her something wasn't right. She needed to find out what in the hell was going on. She was going to finish her investigation. Right now, the woman in the hospital could help her very much. She threw the pillow aside and went to the shower.

As the water spilled over her body, her thoughts went to Malcolm once again. She couldn't shake his touch on her body, his lips on hers as his tongue slid around in her mouth. She had to snap out of this. Her undivided attention was needed on this investigation.

As Grant waited at the terminal for Malcolm's plane to come in, he looked forward to taking Sharon to the show that night. Turns out she was a huge Grim Reaper fan. He'd learned a lot about her life in the hours they spent together. The talked into the night, telling each other about their pasts, the ups and downs. But mostly he chose to linger on the present and future. He was falling for her already and hated the fact that she would eventually have to go back to California.

"Grant!" Malcolm yelled into his ear. He'd said his name several times with no response.

Grant jumped and held his chest. "You can give someone a heart attack like that," he said, pulling himself together.

"I doubt it," said Malcolm. "Where were you, in outer space?"

"Whatever do you mean?" Grant replied, helping Malcolm with his bags.

"Don't play dumb with me. Who is she?"

"I really have no idea what you're talking about," said Grant.

"Fine. If you want to tell me, you'll tell me."

"Well, don't give up so easily. She is a beautiful woman I met yesterday. And she'll be joining me backstage at the show tonight."

"That's what I thought," Malcolm said smartly.

"Oh, and she's a big fan of yours."

Malcolm's smug grin faded and he covered his eyes with his hand and shook his head.

# Chapter Sixteen

At the bar where June had picked up the stranger, Brenna got a little information, but only after shelling out some heavy bucks. She heard terms like "bouncer-looking dude" and "big motorcycle". Although she thanked them for the information, the visit didn't make her feel any better. It all still pointed to Malcolm.

She had to rethink this. The bartender described how happy June seemed with him, and how friendly he'd seemed. That sounded like the Malcolm Brenna knew, and not a fiend capable of rape and murder. Her heart told her one thing while her head told her another.

The hotel clerk, Mr. King, was a bit more help. June had been staying there for a month, having broken up with a boyfriend. She'd come to Houston to live, at his invitation, but he'd failed to tell her he had a wife. June was saving up money to move back home.

Mr. King told her about the night of the attack, saying she'd arrived with a big biker and they couldn't keep their hands off each other. He'd heard a lot of happy noises coming from the room. Brenna blushed at that statement. She then asked if anything strange happened between the time he left and the time he came back.

"Come back?" asked Mr. King. "He didn't come back! At least it didn't seem like the same fellow. See, I have an eye for detail."

"What makes you think it wasn't the same man?" She waited anxiously for any clue that could help clear Malcolm.

"Well, I did tell the police I thought it was the same man because he came back the next day lookin' for her. Asked me all sorts of questions. Then he rushed outta here to get to the hospital. I called the police quick. Told'em he was lookin' for the girl." He was scratching his head.

"Mr. King? You said you didn't think it was the same person after all. What makes you think that?"

"Oh yeah! The details! It was a different bike. He left on a black one and came back on a red one. Had flames on it, and a demon or somethin'."

Brenna thanked him for the information and headed straight for the hospital. Once there, she found out that June had been released to her family and her contact information could not be given.

Brenna thought back to all of these cases and realized there was one more city she needed to visit for information. Phoenix, Arizona.

After returning to the motel, Brenna checked her messages. One was from Malcolm saying he was in Phoenix for a show and would call her soon. Another was from Grant asking her to call him back.

"Grant speaking."

"I'm returning your call," said Brenna.

"Hey, I've been trying to reach you, see how you're doing, but I keep getting your voicemail. Are you okay?"

"I'm in Houston on a case."

"Houston? That's pretty far for a case."

"Actually, I'm going even farther than that. I'm headed for Phoenix. Do you mind if I stay with you?"

"Of course, you can. Tell me when you're coming in. Maybe I can pick you up from the airport."

Malcolm heard the tail end of the conversation, and was curious who he was talking to, but didn't ask.

Grant had sensed there was something brewing between Malcolm and Brenna ever since he'd introduced them; something he had no control over. It bothered him at first, but he'd come to realize that in fact maybe they were a far better match than he and Brenna ever were. Maybe Brenna was the one Malcolm needed in his life. He didn't mention the caller to Malcolm. He would just let it be a little surprise.

# Chapter Seventeen

Brenna laid on the bed resting after all the traveling. She wore a bikini and felt the cool breeze from the fan flowing over her body. She felt pressure on the bed as if someone was joining her. She opened her eyes and was staring into another's. Her first instinct was to run away, but her heart told her no. Her body obeyed, as he moved over her. He brushed her lips with his. She couldn't resist him, she responded by parting her mouth, welcoming his long thick tongue inside.

He had waited so long to have her in the right place and at the right time. He explored every inch of her mouth, entwining their tongues, savoring the sweet taste of her. He moved his hands up and down her body. She wrapped her hands tightly around his neck and surrendered herself to him. He pulled the bikini top off and took her nipple into his mouth and she squealed—

"Miss, are you all right?" asked the flight attendant.

Embarrassed, she sunk down in her seat, hiding her face behind a magazine. She didn't notice the big man who'd come to sit across from her, until he spoke.

"Bad dream?" he asked.

She looked up to him from behind the magazine. To her surprise, he was as big as Malcolm.

"I know what's going through that pretty head of yours," he laughed. "He's a big one!"

Brenna closed her mouth. She had to apologize for her rudeness. "Please accept my apology, sir. It's just that you remind me of someone I know." She continued to stare without realizing it.

Except for the blonde hair and blue eyes, he could almost be Malcolm's twin. The man smiled at her as she continued her assessment.

"Like what ya' see?" he asked. "I hope so, 'cause Miss Lady, I really do like what I see," he said sweetly.

She smiled at the compliment.

"And that fella of yours that I look so much like, you tell him that I said, if he don't treat you right, I just might take you away from him. You're a jewel that he should be sure to take care of." He sat back and smiled in such a way that Brenna felt a chill go through her body.

She didn't have time to respond when the announcement came over the intercom that the plane was arriving at Phoenix and everyone had to buckle their seat belts. Brenna gave one last glance at this man before looking out the window as they made their descent.

Outside the airport doors, Brenna scanned the area, waiting for Grant's car to pull up. She was oblivious to the fact that she had been followed. A large hand suddenly reached out for her, grabbing her arm and pulling her through the crowd rapidly. It happened so fast, and didn't have time to ascertain who it was. She tried to struggle as he forced her into a car. Then she saw him. "Grant!" she yelled heatedly. "You son of a bitch!"

# Chapter Eighteen

"Brenna! Brenna! What has gotten into you?" said Grant, trying to duck her blows inside the car. "It was just a prank. You've never gotten this angry before."

He finally captured her arms and held them down. But she began to cry hysterically. Grant brought her close to his chest and began stroking her gently, speaking soothing and comforting words to her. "Brenna, what's going on here? Why are you so upset? What has happened to you?" He knew Brenna. She was a strong woman. She never broke down like this.

She leaned into him for his strength. She knew that Grant wouldn't stop pressing until he knew what was going on with her. But she didn't want him to hear any suspicions about Malcolm. It would kill him to think his friend was a suspect. And it would hurt him even worst to know he had tried to kill her.

"I'm all right," she said, sitting up at last. "It's just this case I'm working on. It has me paranoid and worked up."

She didn't look at him because he could tell when she was lying. "And then I met this weird man on the plane. He could pass for Malcolm's twin. It was the way he spoke to me, about taking me away from the man I said he reminded me of." She paused as if actually reliving that moment. "And I took it as flirtation, but the way he looked at me and the way he sounded gave me chills. So, when you grabbed me, I thought I was being kidnapped."

"I'm sorry, Brenna. Let's go home."

## Chapter Nineteen

Grant and Brenna made it back to the ranch. He showed her around, inside and out, and introduced her to his horses: a ten-year-old Arabian named Granger; a three-year-old pinto named Sassie; and finally, one-year-old Lucifer, a palomino that Grant described as "crazy as a lunatic". He said he wasn't quite broken in yet and wasn't sure he would ever be.

Brenna was amazed at how much work he had done to the place and complimented him on how nice it looked. He was proud of himself too, walking around with his chest stuck out, agreeing that he had done a pretty good job.

She just laughed at his antics, knowing he was trying to cheer her up.

He showed her to her room and informed her that he had an appointment he needed to keep. She raised a brow as he seemed very vague about this appointment. She watched from the window as he went to his truck with a little pep in his step, and whistling as he went along.

"Hmm. He seems very happy about this appointment. I wonder who she is," she said with a smile.

Brenna unpacked and decided to take a shower. There was a bathroom down the hall, but she used the master bath out of old habit. She stepped into the shower, allowing the steamy waters to soothe her stressed muscles.

Malcolm drove up, not seeing Grant when he left. It had been a hard workout at the arena. He was tired and sweaty. He went to his room and removed his clothes to take a shower. Wrapped in a towel, he went down the hall to the bathroom.

When Brenna finished showering, and with Grant gone to his appointment, she went to the living room to turned on some music.

She sauntered comfortably around the room, knowing she was alone and threw off the towel. She laid down on the couch and stretched out, relaxing to the music.

At the same time the music started, Malcolm had turned on the shower and stepped quickly under it. He washed himself as he thought of Brenna and wondered where she was now. She wasn't answering his calls, and when he'd called her motel in Houston, they said she'd checked out. He was starting to get concerned.

He stepped out of the shower after turning it off. He heard the music coming from the living room. Thinking it must be Grant, he wrapped a towel around him and emerged from the bathroom heading toward the music.

He came around the corner and paused as he looked upon the beautiful sight before him. She didn't know there were eyes fixed on her, as she had drifted to sleep.

## Chapter Twenty

Malcolm couldn't believe his eyes. He approached her and wondered why Grant didn't tell him she was coming. Now he knew who Grant was talking to on the phone the other morning. He touched her face with the back of his hand, softly, and she began to stir. He pulled back for a moment, then he touched her lips with his and she shifted and mumbled his name.

She was dreaming about him. In the dream she was standing before him when he pulled her close for a hungry kiss. She pressed into his body, urging him for more and he gently caressed her. She bent her head back and whispered his name.

Malcolm stared at her in wonderment, hearing her repeatedly call his name. He covered her mouth with his and kissed her hard and she swung her arms around his neck in response, pulling him closer. He picked her up to take her to his room.

But Brenna felt herself being lifted and suddenly awoke. The first moment she was happy to be in his arms, and then reality hit her and she began to panic. She realized she was undressed and also remembered the other night. Her fears came flooding back. "Put me down!" she screamed.

Malcolm was confused. She seemed terrified of him. "Brenna, darlin' what–"

He never finished because she slapped him as hard as she could to get him to release her. It worked. She hit the floor and then ran to her room and locked it. She leaned against the door, scared that she had just made him angry and sealed her own fate.

Malcolm needed answers. He knocked on her door. "Brenna! What is wrong with you?"

She jumped back at the sound of his voice. She was fearful, but also felt something else. She both did and didn't want him in.

"Look girl," he said, "I'm a patient man, but I have my limits. Tell me what's wrong! You and I almost had something going the last time I saw you. What have I done that's so drastic to change that in such a short time?" He was more confused than ever.

"Just go away Malcolm, please!"

She turned to the bed to throw herself on it, when the door crashed open. There stood a very angry Malcolm.

96

Brenna couldn't breathe.

# Chapter Twenty-One

Malcolm stood still momentarily, watching Brenna as she trembled next to the bed. He made a step toward her and she moved back into the bed with terror in her eyes. He looked at her with such confusion and pain. Finally, their eyes locked on each other's.

They were both confused at what was happening, but for different reasons. An overwhelming sensation flowed between them. Brenna was having mixed emotions. She couldn't decide if this man was a killer or the man she had fallen for. Malcolm helped her make that decision.

Without another thought, he bridged the gap between them and she was in his arms. Before she could make any protest, his mouth had claimed hers. At first, she wanted to object, but she couldn't. She could only give in.

Her breath was now shallow and rapid. He was at her throat now, pecking softly, then licking and sucking. She groaned at the feel of his lips on her. She let out a small squeal as his mouth closed around her nipple and his hand engulfed her breast, kneading and massaging. He was making her wetter with every passing second.

He lifted her up and she wrapped her legs around his waist. She couldn't believe that just moments ago she'd ordered him to go away.

Malcolm laid her on the bed and threw his towel away. She scooted back on her elbows, gasping at the size of him. He moved onto the bed, approaching her like an animal stalking his prey. She was the meal he desired now.

He hovered over her and stared down into her eyes. Now they showed the same burning fires that he felt. She pulled him forcefully closer and he gave himself to her, knowing at last that she would be his forever.

As they slept in each other's arms, Brenna had twirled a lock of his hair around her fingers and laid her head peacefully on Malcolm's chest. He'd awoken first, but remained still as not to wake her. When her eyes did flutter open. He asked how she was feeling, in a gentle voice. He stroked her cheek with his hand and she looked up into his eyes and smiled.

"I'm feeling wonderful, Malcolm," she said.

"Good," he whispered and delicately stroked her cheek.

She'd made up her mind. She knew in her heart he was innocent, and she was going to prove it no matter what she had to do.

She released his hair and rose from his arms. She covered his body with kisses and tender bites. Then she climbed over his body. She didn't have to wait as he was ready for her. They joined together and soon they were moving in rhythm. Then, just as both thought they would lose control, he flipped her over to her back and thrust even deeper inside her.

"Malcolm, I love you," she breathed, and she knew she'd never uttered truer words.

Hearing this brought Malcolm to the very apex of pleasure. They came together in an explosion of love, frustration, fear, pain, doubts, and all the feelings they had endured since the day they cast their eyes on each other. Then they plummeted to the earth, spent of every bit of energy and laid in each other's arms, fulfilled at last.

# Chapter Twenty-Two

Malcolm had just begun to stir when he heard Grant's truck driving up. He looked around at the clock and realized time was late and he needed to get to the arena. Malcolm looked down at Brenna lying next to him deep in sleep. Not wanting to arouse her, he slowly eased out of the bed, retrieved his towel and wrapped it around his waist. He smiled down on the dark beauty lying so peacefully in the bed. He gave her a light kiss on the lips, and paused when she slightly moved. When she settled down, he turned and walked to the door.

Not wanting to be found in a compromising situation, he left her room quietly and closed the door. Fortunately, the door still clicked into its now slightly-cracked frame. He'd figure out a way to explain that later. He went to the bathroom to get ready for the night.

Grant opened the front door and allowed Sharon to enter before him, showing his gentlemanly ways. She was very impressed with the home already.

"Very lovely place you have here, Grant."

"Thank you. I'm glad you approve."

Grant felt his heart flutter. She had the prettiest, most seductive brown eyes. He leaned in for a kiss and she welcomed it.

Brenna woke and put on her robe. She wondered where Malcolm had gone and went in search of him. When she heard the shower going, she smiled devilishly and made her way to the bathroom. She quietly opened the door, slipped out of her robe and eased her way into the shower behind him.

His head was under the running water and he jumped when he felt her smooth small arms encircle him. He quickly grabbed them, and turned to gaze at her. He really appreciated her initiative and smiled in approval. "As much as I would love to take you here and now," he said with a seductive growl, "trust me when I say this is not the time or place for this." He then gave her a gentle kiss on the lips.

"I see, you want to play hard to get," said Brenna. She brought herself closer to him and rubbed her hands on his silky wet chest.

"No, baby. I would never play hard to get with you. Grant is here, and he's brought his new lady friend."

She quickly jumped out of the shower throwing on her robe, looked down the hallway to see if the coast was clear, and ran to her room. Malcolm just smiled and shook his head, leaning back against the wall and thought of how much he wished Grant was still gone. He made a mental note that they would finish this one soon.

After dressing, Brenna went downstairs and was introduced to Sharon. She could immediately feel the chemistry between the two and hoped that this could be a really good thing for Grant. "Any friend of Grant's is a friend of mine," she told Sharon.

"Thanks Brenna. You don't know how good that makes me feel," she said, receiving Brenna's hand.

Shortly after, Malcolm descended the stairs. "Well, Grant, do I get to meet this pretty lady?"

Sharon remained composed, but inside she was very excited to meet the Grim Reaper himself. She didn't want to appear like a crazed fan, so she politely waited for Grant to introduce them. Malcolm never gave him the chance. He passed Grant and took Sharon's hand and kissed it.

Sharon was speechless as her hand was engulfed in his, his lips touching it softly. Inside she was screaming, her heart was pounding fiercely, but on the outside, she was only calm and courteous.

"Well, people. I've got to get to the arena. I'll see you two there," he said to Grant and Sharon. "And I'll see you later too," he said to Brenna with a secret wink.

After he was gone, Sharon revealed her true feelings. "That was Grim Reaper! My favorite wrestler! You didn't tell me you knew Grim Reaper. No one will believe this. I actually saw him up close and personal. Oh, Grant, thank you!" She wrapped her arms around his neck and kissed him long and hard.

Brenna slipped away, leaving the two in privacy.

# Chapter Twenty-Three

Brenna went to the local police department she once worked for. She was greeted with love. It was like a family reunion. She was able to convince them to let her look over a particular file.

But someone was watching her very closely and wasn't happy to see Brenna. "What brings you here, Sims?"

The familiar voice referring to her by her last name made Brenna cringe. "Lynne Powell, you're still here? Then things haven't gotten better around here after all. They're still the same."

"I see you're still a bitch," said Lynne.

"Look, Powell, I'm here on official business. Now if you're having a bad day go take it out on someone else." Brenna glared at the woman who was once her partner.

"Official business? Don't make me laugh. You're nothing but a lowly dick."

"But a good dick," Brenna said with a grin.

"Let me give you a warning. I'm lieutenant now. So, if you're thinking of coming back, forget it."

Brenna didn't see the emotion come over Lynne as she left the room. She sat for a few moments and thought about how close they once were. Seemed so long ago. She turned back to the file and spotted what she was looking for.

Grant and Sharon had waited as long as they could for Brenna, thinking she might want to attend the show too, but it was getting late, so Grant gave her a call. She said she would meet them there as she had one more thing to take care of.

When Brenna hung up, she was about to enter her car when she saw Lynne staring at her from the station. They shared glances for a moment, Lynne turned and went back inside. Brenna looked down momentarily, then unlocked her car. There was one more piece of info she needed and she would have to visit the library.

Lynne came over to the policeman who had the file Brenna had reviewed. She took it into her office and looked over it thoroughly. She wondered why, after so much time, Brenna would be interested in this dead issue. She planned to find out.

Brenna found an archived newspaper at the library that had the information she was looking for. She took down the information and left for the arena. But Lynne had tracked her down in the library. She retrieved the paper Brenna had read and wondered again why she was re-opening this can of worms.

As Brenna drove down the road, she considered going back to the ranch to change into something more dazzling for Malcolm, but she was only a couple of miles from the arena. So, she drove on.

Suddenly, the car sputtered and stopped. The gas tank was full, the car was new. She couldn't figure it out. She thought of calling Grant but realized he would be on his way to the show by now. She decided to walk the distance. She would see if all her workouts had paid off.

She had walked only a little way when she heard the unmistakable sound of a motorcycle approaching. She stopped in her tracks and turned to look. Her mind went to the possibility that someone may have tampered with her car. There was nowhere to hide in this open space. Still, she needed to get off the road. If she started running now, maybe the rider wouldn't notice her and would go on by. She could make it to a house for help.

The motorcycle was rapidly approaching and she took off. She scaled a short fence and ran through a field. She heard the motorcycle pause behind her for a few moments, but she didn't turn around. He must have spotted her. She ran faster, as if her life depended on it. And as far as she was concerned it did. Then she heard the bike speed the other direction. Stopping to catch her breath, she sat down. When she rose to her feet again, she saw the person on the motorcycle.

Gripped with fear, she looked around for some type of hiding place, hoping he had not spotted her. It was too late. He revved up his engine and started toward her. She ran but soon the bike rolled up beside her.

Suddenly, she felt the large arm encircle her waist and lift her onto the bike. She fought the person and screamed, but none of it seemed to have an effect. She realized how similar he was to Malcolm and as her life unfolded before her She regretted having ever thought that Malcolm could be guilty, and that she had kept her investigation a secret from those close to her. Now she would go to her death and there was no one around to help.

# Chapter Twenty-Four

Brenna turned to get a good look at the man who was speeding away with her, but she couldn't see his eyes. He had on dark glasses, a bandanna, and a long coat with a hood over his head.

The man never spoke a word. He kept his eyes fix ahead as he drove into the city. She presumed he would take her to some alley way and dispose of her.

Tears began to pour out of her eyes. The wind whipped past her face. Stricken with fear, Brenna clung to the jacket of the man who would take her to an unknown place and do to her what he had done to the other women. She closed her eyes and prayed that some miracle help would come her way.

Soon they came to a big building and went down into an underground garage. It was barely lit, but as they went further in, it became very evident where they were. Her body went limp and she fainted.

Malcolm could barely make out the figure coming toward him in the dim concrete corridor, but he immediately recognized Brenna in the man's arms. "What happened?" Malcolm cried.

"Man, I do you a favor and what do you give me? Not one 'thank you'!" Lance snapped as he laid her carefully in Malcolm's arms.

"You're right," said Malcolm, his eyes never leaving Brenna's face. "Thank you. What happened?"

Still wearing his sunglasses and hood, Lance spoke more softly then before, but Malcolm didn't notice. He was too worried about Brenna. As they hurried down the hallway, Lance tried to explain. "I saw her running across the field. I figured she needed help. Then I recognized her. But she gave me one glance and took off running again. I figured she'd mistaken me for a stalker or something. So, I revved up my bike and grabbed her up like in one of those old western movies."

For a moment, Malcolm thought that Lance's voice sounded strange, but he couldn't think about that right now. "Did you tell her who you were?"

"Man, I couldn't talk to her, she was hysterical," said Lance as he folded his arms across his chest.

Malcolm shook his head. "Thank you for bringing her to me, but you've got some issues you need to see about."

Lance's eyes narrowed.

Malcolm entered his dressing room carrying Brenna and Grant and Sharon panicked. "What happened? Is she all right?"

"I think so. She just fainted. She was scared half to death by a friend of mine." He laid her on the couch and Sharon went to the table to get some water.

"Watch her, Grant," said Malcolm. "I'm going to get some help." He laid a hand on Grant's shoulder and then left. And the look of concern on Malcolm's face revealed his true feelings for Brenna.

# Chapter Twenty-Five

A car pulled beside Brenna's and the occupant stepped out and looked around. Not seeing anyone about, they went over to the car, took a look inside, found her purse and went through it. Then they left with her driver's license in-hand.

Brenna finally began to stir as Malcolm stroked her cheek with the back of his hand. Grant stood behind him with his arm around Sharon, waiting anxiously. Soon she opened her eyes and her gaze fell on Malcolm.

Her mind becoming clear, she began to panic, remembering the ordeal she'd just been through. Malcolm took her into his arms as she caught her breath.

"Oh, Malcolm! I've been such a fool! I should have told all of you what has been happening!" She began to cry.

"Maybe we should leave," said Sharon. "I'll take her home. She is in no shape to be here tonight."

"Wait," said Malcolm. "What do you mean about telling us what's been going on?" Malcolm pulled Brenna slightly away from him and stared into her eyes.

"Oh, Reaper, can't this wait? She needs to be at home resting," Sharon pleaded.

Malcolm turned and glared at Sharon, and just as quickly his stare softened when he realized she was just trying to be helpful. But most of all, she was right. Brenna needed to be home resting. "She's right, Brenna. Sharon's going to take you home. Will you be all right?"

"Yes. Maybe a nice shower and bed will do me some good." She looked softly into Malcolm's concerned eyes. "But tomorrow I have something I need to tell you. All of you."

"I'm going with you," said Grant. He had a foreboding feeling in the pit of his stomach. Something wasn't right here. He'd known Brenna for years, as both a friend and a lover. She had nerves of steel. Why would she get so hysterical from someone coming to assist her?

"No Grant, it's okay," said Brenna. "You stay with Malcolm and enjoy the show and come back together. I'll take this time to get to know Sharon."

"Yes," Sharon agreed. "It'll be girl's night in."

"Take my car," said Malcolm giving them the keys.

Malcolm was a little surprised when Brenna took him by the shoulders and pulled him closer for a deep, passionate kiss.

Grant smiled at Sharon. They didn't need any more confirmation than that. They left them alone for a moment and went into the hall. Lance appeared just then. Grant couldn't hold back.

"Lance, Malcolm tells me you've had a real problem lately. What in hell's gotten into you?"

Lance stopped and snarled. "Malcolm needs to mind his own business and keep his sluts in line." He started to walk away.

Grant started behind him, but Sharon grabbed his arm. Grant touched her hand, letting her know it was all right. "Lance I've known you since Malcolm and I met up again," he said to the man with his back to him. "I always thought highly of you. And Brenna is a fine woman. Malcolm's lucky to have her in his life. So, when you are in my presence, you will address her in a mannerly way. Or you and I will have it out."

Lance shrugged him off and walked away, but not before giving Sharon a sideways stare. She moved behind Grant.

"Who is that man?"

He was surprised she didn't recognize him. "Right. You're used to seeing him with a mask. It's Lance Connors."

"Really?"

# Chapter Twenty-Six

Sharon and Brenna went back to Grant's house and Brenna told Sharon to make herself at home while she went to take a quick shower. She quietly closed the bedroom door behind her and leaned on it for a moment as her mind drifted back to the day's events. She covered her face with her hands and began to let out the outburst of tears she'd been holding back since she'd first regained consciousness. She had been through so much in the last week that she didn't know if she could take any more.

She knew she had to share it all with someone. But who? If she told Malcolm, he'd be hurt that she could have thought him capable of such things. She didn't know Sharon well enough to confide anything of this magnitude to her. And Grant. He had always been so understanding, but no. She couldn't put it all on him alone. She would tell both Malcolm and Grant the truth the next day, as promised, and she would face the consequences. Honesty was the only way.

While Brenna was in the shower, Sharon was busy in the kitchen preparing something for her and Brenna to eat. She was also admiring the way Grant's kitchen was organized. She found everything easily. She paused, when she thought she heard a noise coming from outside. She started to go tell Brenna, but decided she didn't need to be spooked any more that night.

She opened the door and stepped outside to see if she could see anything and she heard the noise again. She went across the porch to peer out to the open field and around the side of the house. Nothing. She saw Grant's dog sleeping quietly on the porch, so she shrugged her shoulders and started back into the house. As she made it to the doorway, she heard a big crash behind her. She turned and screamed.

Lynne stared at the file Brenna had perused earlier. It was the case of a young woman found dead when they were still partners. She found this strange as it was the case that made her decide to leave the force. Why had she come back to dredge it up again?

She looked at the event sheet and wondered what it was Brenna was after. If she knew Brenna, she was on to something that was probably over her head. She took one last glance at the sheet before her. Then it struck her.

Brenna wouldn't have come back to this case unless she thought the new ones were connected.

She closed up her files and gathered her things. She had to see Brenna. And she knew her well enough to know there was a good chance she'd be at Grant's place.

A man gave a quick knock and ducked his head into Malcolm's dressing room. "I'm sorry to bother you, but have you seen, Lance?"

"No Jimmy," said Malcolm. "Haven't seen him in about an hour."

Jimmy looked anxious. "Neither has anybody else," he said angrily and stormed away.

"I guess Lance got lost," said Malcolm.

Grant chuckled as he flipped through a magazine. "He's lost all right. He was acting like a real asshole to Sharon and me."

"You know something," said Malcolm. "It's not like Lance to disappear during a show, and it's not like him to act the way he has been lately. Something's seriously wrong, and he won't tell me anything."

"He sure as hell hasn't been himself," said Grant. "In fact, when he left us, and Sharon asked me who he was, I almost said I didn't know myself."

"What did you just say?" Malcolm asked turning to him.

"When?" Grant was confused.

Malcolm went to Grant and stood over him with a strange look in his eyes. "You said Sharon asked you who Lance was? If she knew me, wouldn't she know Lance as well? Isn't she a long-time fan?"

Grant thought about it for a minute. "That's right," he said. "I guess it is a little strange."

Sharon held her chest, trying to calm herself. Grant's cat had jumped or fallen from the roof and tumbled onto the trash cans. She'd thought her heart would leap right from her rib cage. Regaining her composure, she picked up the cat and stroked its fur.

"What's going on?" asked Brenna who'd come to the doorway.

"Oh, I was a little spooked for a moment," said Sharon. "I heard something outside, but it turned out to be the cat."

Brenna was relieved. "That cat is a menace," she laughed as Sharon followed her inside. "And you certainly know your way around a kitchen," she said. "Something smells delicious."

When Sharon's Swedish meatballs were done, she moved them to a platter and Brenna prepared some cheese and fruit and poured them both some brandy. They sat back on the couch to relax and enjoy. They were quiet for a while until Brenna broke the silence.

"How much longer will you be here?" she asked.

"I'm not sure," said Sharon. "But it's going to be hard to leave."

"You and Grant are hitting it off that good, huh?" Brenna asked with a knowing smile.

"Yeah, we are," Sharon admitted. "But I hope the long distance doesn't put a damper on things."

"Don't worry," said Brenna. "I'm sure it'll work out."

Sharon looked comforted, but then she put down her glass and her look became a little more serious. "Do you mind if I ask you something?"

"I don't mind," Brenna replied.

"Why were you so frightened of the man they called Lance?"

"I don't know," said Brenna. "I was stranded and he showed up on his bike and then followed me when I ran across the field. Then he chased me down and grabbed me." Brenna had turned her eyes. She didn't want Sharon to know her initial reasons for being afraid and having run in the first place.

"He chased you down?"

"Yeah."

"Why didn't he just identify himself? The Lance I know–" Sharon paused and went to get herself another to drink from the bar.

"That's right," Brenna said, "You are a longtime wrestling fan." She couldn't see the sadness in Sharon's eyes.

"Why do they think that man is Lance?" Sharon asked.

Brenna was beginning to feel a buzz from the brandy. She couldn't register Sharon's last remark. And even more, since she wasn't a fan, she didn't know Lance from Adam. Sharon returned to the couch and sat next to Brenna whose eyes were a little blood-shot.

"Brenna, I think you should slow down," she laughed. "We have the whole night until the boys get here." Sharon took what was left in the glass from Brenna and sat it to the side.

"You're right," said Brenna. "I'm going to go put some water on my face."

Sharon received a notification on her phone. She stepped out onto the porch for some privacy and made a call. While waiting through several rings, she noticed the dog was no longer on the porch. She gazed all around and decided he must have run into the field. Just then, her call was answered.

Malcolm and Grant were both deep in thought. Grant wondered why Sharon hadn't recognized Lance and then remembered the eerie feeling he'd had at first about the girls going home alone.

Malcolm paced back and forth, pushing back his hair, his mind going over everything that had happened over the past few weeks. Lance had been acting very strangely. He remembered the woman who'd been beaten badly, and that Lance had come in with scratches and bruises like he'd been in a fight. He remembered having to explain to the police that he himself had nothing to do with the crime. And he learned that a man had arrived at the scene on a motorcycle and fitting his own general description. Then he learned that Lance could in fact ride, contrary to what he'd always known. Then Lance terrorized Brenna. Now he was missing.

He turned to Grant who seemed to be going through a dilemma of his own. "What's on your mind?" Malcolm asked.

"I don't know what it is, but something is really wrong here, man. And it's got something to do with Lance."

"I agree. He hasn't been himself lately. It's like he's someone else altogether."

"And Brenna," said Grant. "It's like she is on the verge of a breakdown. I've never seen her so fragile before."

Malcolm folded his arms across his chest as he stroked his chin. "How do you mean?" he asked.

"I mean, she was a police detective with the department here, and now she's a P.I. Does that sound like someone who would panic just because someone on a motorcycle stopped to give her a hand?"

"No, but Lance did chase her down and grab her."

"Yeah. That's pretty messed up. And I think these things are connected somehow."

"Brenna said she had something to tell us tomorrow," Malcolm remembered. "Maybe we should talk to her tonight."

Grant agreed. "There are some other things I'd like to clear up too. Like why Sharon didn't recognize Lance."

"He does sometimes wear a mask," said Malcolm. "And maybe she's just not as big a fan as you thought."

Grant shook his head. "Nah. There's some other reason, and I want to know what it is."

Malcolm agreed. "You know what? I think we need to get back to your place. I have a pressing feeling that we're needed there." He grabbed his bag and the two men went immediately out the door.


When Brenna returned, she didn't see Sharon, so she went to the kitchen to look for her. She didn't see her but did hear her talking outside and guessed that the guys had come back early. But when she neared the door, she realized Sharon's was the only voice. She must be on the phone. Brenna smiled to herself and turned away, but then she heard something that froze her in place.

"I'm here with her now," she'd heard Sharon say. "This may create a problem."

Brenna was listening very closely now.

"Are you sure she was looking over the same information?" Sharon said into the phone. "I can't have her getting in the way of my plans. This has to go off without a hitch. We need her out of the way! I'll have to take care of her myself. Well, that sounds good to me. See you later."

Sharon hung up the phone, paused for a moment, and then entered the house. She found Brenna sitting quietly on the couch. She didn't have a clue that Brenna had heard her conversation, and Brenna certainly wasn't going to mentioned it. At least not yet.

"Can I ask you a question?" Sharon asked, sitting next to Brenna.

"Sure."

"The dog. Has he ever run off before?"

"As far as I know he's very lazy," Brenna replied. "He doesn't wander far unless he is with someone." Brenna watched as Sharon stared strangely in the direction of the back porch. She curious as to why Sharon would be so concerned about the dog, but just now she wanted to find out some other things about this woman.

"I understand you were once a police detective here in Phoenix," said Sharon.

Brenna nodded, figuring Grant had told the woman.

"And now you're a P.I.?" Sharon asked.

Brenna was getting a little nervous and wondered what this line of questioning was leading to.

Sharon narrowed her eyes this time. "Been on any good cases lately?"

"You know, Sharon, we've been talking about me all this time. Tell me something about you."

"First," said Sharon. "There's something I think we should take care of before the boys get here." She then stood and went to her purse.

Brenna got up. Fear gripped her as she watched Sharon reach into the bag. She was pulling something out when the lights suddenly went black. Brenna heard movement and thought Sharon was coming toward her. Then she heard a thump, a small whimper, and then a thud hit the floor.

"Sharon, are you all right?" she called out.

No one responded.

She moved as quickly as she could through the darkness to the kitchen. She'd get some candles.

"Sharon?" she called again. Again, no response.

She was frightened, but also wondered if Sharon had hurt herself. She continued to move to the kitchen and she bumped into someone huge. She started to scream when she felt a sharp pain in the top of her head. Then blackness claimed her.

# Chapter Twenty-Seven

On her way to Grant's ranch to look for Brenna, Lynne made a quick stop home to take a look at some documents she had there. They were in regards to a current case she'd been working on the FBI was now involved in. She thought about Brenna's last case in Phoenix and how she'd said she'd left because of it. Of course, she always believed that Grant Mitchum was the real reason she'd left. Having been partners and close friends, Lynne knew that their feelings for each other were not the same and that Grant wouldn't accept it.

Then she found what she was looking for. Same M.O. as the other cases. It all fit together. She quickly dialed a certain FBI agent who would want to know. Then she hurried to her car and continued to her destination.

Brenna slowly stirred from unconsciousness and felt a pounding headache. She gently cradled her head between her hands. Light penetrated her eyes and a blurry image before her soon became sharp. She looked into the terror-stricken eyes of Sharon who was sitting near her on the couch.

Sharon was also holding her head, but with a small bag of ice. Her eyes then led Brenna to look at someone else who was seated in a chair right across from them. Brenna's eyes widened in shock and she sat up fast. "You!" she exclaimed.

Sharon touched her arm gently to calm her down.

"Yes, me," said Lance. "How are you feeling?"

Brenna stared at him hard. Was Lance the killer? Suddenly, her head throbbed even more.

"I see I must have put a little more strength into that pop on the head than I'd planned." He left his seat to get her a bag of ice.

"Look, Brenna," Sharon whispered. "I was going to tell you something before the lights went out. I need you not to get this man upset." She started to say more, but Lance re-entered the room.

"It's not nice to whisper," he said. "I might think you're talking about me, and I might get angry. And ladies, that is not what you want."

He handed Brenna the bag of ice.

"Why are you doing this to us?" Brenna asked.

"Why am I doing this to you? Well, you two have been very naughty girls, snooping around."

"What are you talking about?" Brenna asked, looking at both Lance and Sharon.

Lance eased back into his seat. "You two were digging into a case that happened a year ago. You're very meddlesome." Lance smiled deviously and noticed the confusion on Brenna's face as she looked at Sharon.

"Oh, you didn't know?" he laughed.

"I didn't know what?" asked Brenna.

"Your little friend here is not all she seems to be."

Grant stared through the window as they drove out of the city. He had a lot on his mind. "Malcolm, this feeling that something is wrong is really getting to me. And there's something else too. It's Sharon. Maybe she's mixed up in it."

"Hold on, Grant. What brought this on? Don't tell me it's because she didn't know who Lance was. Hell, I've been wondering who he is my damned self."

Then Malcolm began to recall how strangely Brenna had acted before they made love. "Grant, something just occurred to me. Brenna's gonna kill me for saying anything, but there's a reason I have to tell you."

"Yeah," said Grant, still taking in the scenery.

"Well, today, Brenna and I slept together." He was about to continue, but Grant's head snapped around fast and he shifted in the seat to hear more.

"Look, man, I'm not revealing any details. So, you might as well forget it."

"I got you," said Grant with a satisfied grin.

Malcolm chuckled. "Anyway, today when we were alone, before things happened, she saw me and panicked. She was truly afraid of me; even when I tried to talk to her. It was so strange, because the other night everything was cool."

"That's what I mean, man," said Grant. "Ever since she's been on this case, she's been jumpy."

"Do you know what case she's on?"

"No. She never tells me anything."

"But getting back to Sharon, follow your gut, Grant. That's what she'll end up doing. If you doubt her, she'll feel it. What does your gut tell you?"

"That I love her," he admitted.


"What do you mean, she isn't what she seems to be?" Brenna asked. Lance just sat smugly in his chair with his arms crossed, so Brenna turned to Sharon. "What does he mean? Are you in on this with him? I heard you tell–"

Sharon didn't let her finish. "I know you heard me say that I had something to talk to you about," she lied in front of Lance. "And what he's trying to tell you is what I was going to tell you *very soon.*"

Maybe it was her years as a detective, but Brenna quickly realized that Sharon was trying to tell her something more than what her lips were saying. Her eyes told her that the person Sharon had been speaking to on the phone was on their way to help. So, Brenna played along and didn't finish her previous sentence.

"Okay," she said. "Then tell me now. What is Lance trying to tell me about you?"

"That I'm an FBI agent," Sharon replied.

# Chapter Twenty-Eight

Brenna was stunned. Her head started to throb again. "I don't understand," she said.

"You and I are on the same case," said Sharon.

Brenna's mind began to reel. She looked at Sharon realizing this really could be the man they were looking for.

Sharon nodded.

Brenna's blood ran cold again as she returned her stare to Lance. "You're trying to frame Malcolm?" she asked. She remained calm. She would have to push her fears aside. She needed answers. "But he's your friend," she said.

"No!" he shouted. "I'm trying to pay him back. He has never been my friend. He is the reason my girl had to be dealt with. I told her what would happen if she ever messed around on me. She didn't listen." He leaned forward and continued. "That night, I saw her leaving the bar with him. I followed them and waited. After he left, I went to confront her. And you know what? He'd given her money for her time, like she was some cheap whore. And the worst thing about it? She took it, willingly." Lance began to snap. "I couldn't stomach her any longer. After all I'd done to show her how much I loved her… now I had to show her how much I hated her."

He stood and went to the window. To their surprise, he seemed more sad than angry. The women had just heard a motive for the first murder. They would have to guess the reasons for the others, but one thing still didn't make sense to Brenna. "I don't understand why Malcolm would betray him after knowing him so long."

"Because Brenna, he isn't who you think he is," said Sharon. "Remember that I asked why they thought he was Lance? It's because I've known Lance for a long time. And we've kept in touch until a few weeks ago. I haven't heard from him since."

Brenna realized what Sharon was saying and the two women stared into each other's eyes; one was in disbelief, and the other was relieved the truth was out. Then they turned their attention to the man standing at the window. He became anxious when a car could be heard pulling up the drive.

When Lynne had spoken to Sharon earlier by phone, she'd clued her in that Brenna was investigating the same case.

She knew that Brenna wouldn't stop until she solved the case or got killed. They had their differences, but she wouldn't let anything happen to her. Sharon had told her she would take care of Brenna, letting her into their confidence, and ask her to step aside and let them finish the case. They had every reason to believe she would comply. If that didn't work, Lynne would haul her ass to jail under protective custody. As she drove along, she could see a pair of headlights fast approaching in her rear-view mirror.

Malcolm and Grant had remained in silence for most of the trip. Each was in his own world, worrying about the women in their lives. One man was concerned with the emotions of the woman he loved, and the other was worried that his woman might not be all that she seems.

Up ahead they saw another car on the two-lane road. Malcolm decided to pass it, and when he did, Grant got a look at the driver. He did a double-take. "Malcolm, stop!"

His yell caused Malcolm to swerve before regaining control and bringing the car to a halt in the middle of the road. The other car was blocked. Grant didn't explain. He jumped out and waived his arms at the other car as he approached it.

The two women froze. Brenna worried that Malcolm and Grant had just pulled into the driveway and that this maniac would kill them. She had to think of something.

The man turned to the women and gave them a smile. "I'm going out here to greet our company," he said. "If one of you tries to escape, I will kill the other one. If you both try, I promise that neither of you will make it off this ranch alive. And I keep my promises." His last chilling remark was an eerie reminder to both detectives. He gave them one last cryptic glance and went out the door.

"Brenna, listen to me. Lieutenant Powell and I are working together. She followed you around when she discovered you were investigating this case. She is on her way here to help me convince you to back off. That may be her out there now." Sharon kept her eyes pinned in the door.

"Lynne? No—"

"If we play it cool, we may be able to get out of this alive."

"Sharon, you're certain he is not Lance?"

Sharon nodded. "Yes."

"Then where is Lance?"

"He's right here," the imposter said, re-entering the room. This time he was accompanied by two other men. One was bound at the wrists. The other was making sure he didn't get away. The imposter shoved the bound man onto the couch between the two women.

Sharon gasped and hugged the man. This one was obviously Lance. Brenna was surprised to see him and the imposter at the same time. They looked very much alike. It was evident that Lance had been beaten. There were old cuts and bruises on his face, and one eye was bluish-purple.

The man who'd arrived with him went to Brenna and stood towering over her. "I told you to tell that man of yours that if he didn't know how to treat you, I'd be more than happy to take you off his hands."

Brenna had a vile, nauseating feeling when she realized he was the man she'd met on the plane. He reached out to touch her and she jumped back and into Lance. Lance tried to lunge at the man, even though his wrists were still bound, but Sharon grabbed him and urged him to stop.

"I guess our last encounter didn't teach you nothin', did it, Lance?" The imposter gave him a brutal back-hand slap. A burning red print marked his face. The women screamed out, but Lance didn't make a sound.

"Hey, Bart, quit foolin' around," said the imposter. "Get over here. There's something moving out there."

"Lance! Are you all right?" Sharon whispered. "They've had you all this time? All of these weeks?" she asked, gently caressing his cheek.

"No," he said. "They didn't get me until a couple of nights ago. Malcolm and I had a falling out about something. I followed him to the bar and was going to smooth things over with him, when I saw him go over to you." He turned around to face Brenna.

"So, I waited for a while, but when I saw the two of you leave on his bike, I started for home. That's when I was jumped and kidnapped. Then, that son-of-a- bitch took over my identity. Sharon, I haven't called you for weeks because I knew somebody was following me. I didn't want you to get into any danger yourself. As a matter of fact, they jumped me before, back in Houston, the night he beat up a woman there."

Sharon spoke as quietly as possible. "Lance, do you know anything about them?"

He shook his head. "Just that they're brothers."

Sharon thought for a moment. "You two are aware that we have to get out of here somehow. If we don't, we're dead."

"Man, you're spooked," Bart said to the imposter. "I don't see a thing." He turned from the window and went back toward the couch.

"Ya' know somethin'?" he said to the women while licking his lips. "Both of you are purdy little things. "I think I could have a good time with the both of you. A big man like me has a big appetite. What do ya' think Gus," he asked, revealing the imposter's name. "You think they can satisfy my appetite?" He ran his tongue slowly over his lips, as his eyes began to undress the women.

Lance felt useless. He clenched his teeth. He was ready to burst free of his constraints. He could see the women's fear beginning to show. Sharon leaned further into Lance. Neither woman was sure what would happen now.

"Bart, leave those ladies alone," warned Gus. "I'm waiting for those two to show up, and I need you here when they do. You can do what you want with'em when I'm finished making him pay for Jill's death."

# Chapter Twenty-Nine

"Grant, have you lost your mind?" Lynne yelled, sticking her head out the car window as Grant approached.

"What brings you out this way, Lynne?" he asked, leaning on her car.

"I'm on duty," she said. "I can't get into specifics. And I've got to hurry."

"My ranch is the only property out here for quite a way. Your 'specifics' weren't taking you there, were they? Without a search warrant?" Grant knew something was up. Lynne wouldn't be out this way for nothing.

Just then, Malcolm emerged from the car. Lynne's eyes became large when she noticed his size. He was even larger than Grant. She knew Grant wouldn't let up, and now he had a friend who would no doubt assist him in his persuasion. Then she recognized him. Hell, maybe they could give her some of the information she was looking for. She gave in and got out of the car.

"All right, you win," she said, folding her arms over her chest. "Has Brenna told you anything about the case she's working on?"

"She told me she was on one, but didn't give any details," said Grant.

"Well, unofficially, it's a murder case. And you, Malcolm, are a very important part of this case. Yeah, I know who you are."

"I think you'd better come to the point," said Malcolm. He'd lost his composure. Not only had she just said he was a part of a murder case, but he was still anxious to get back to Brenna.

"Okay, here goes. Malcolm, last year a young woman was found killed in her apartment here in Phoenix. Her name was Jill Spencer. Does that name ring a bell?"

"Should it?" he asked.

"Your company was here when it happened. That young woman reportedly left a bar with you. Tall, slender, fiery red hair, and her eyes were as green as yours." She studied Malcolm closely as she waited for his response.

"I could have met her," he replied. "But I don't remember every woman I meet. I usually only see them once." Then his eyes sparked, as a memory of green eyes formed in his head.

Lynne moved from the car. "You remember something, don't you?" she said. "I don't care how unimportant it may seem to you; I want to know what it is."

"Yeah, I do recall something. She complained about a crazy boyfriend. They'd just broken up and she was out looking for excitement. She was celebrating her freedom."

More memories began to flood his mind. I remember seeing a picture of him on her TV. I didn't look at it good, but he was a big guy. She did tell me he was a biker. She said those are the only guys that attracted her."

Then, Malcolm remembered one last detail and a feeling of dread washed over him. "She said he'd told her he'd kill her if she ever 'messed around on him'."

Grant had an eerie realization. "Seems he made good on that promise," he said mournfully.

"Maybe he did kill her," said Lynne. "But we have other cases where the women are linked to you. That doesn't look too good."

"Wait, a damned minute," Malcolm blasted. "What in the hell do you mean 'women', plural? I was questioned on one case, and it wasn't a murder. When they realized it wasn't me, they let me go," he said angrily. His temper was escalating.

"You are barking up the wrong tree, lieutenant," Grant barked.

"Calm down," said Lynne. "I'm only here to see where this case is going. I'm trying to clear you, Malcolm. I think this is a frame up. I want the real guy, but I need your cooperation."

Lynne went over placed a gentle hand on his arm, with pleading eyes.

"Whatever I can do to clear myself," he said, leaning against her car.

"I know about that case in Houston, Malcolm. I know that the woman told investigators you weren't her attacker. I shouldn't tell you this, but she identified another in a photo lineup. His name was Lance Connors."

"No, it can't be," said Grant.

Lynne noticed that Malcolm's back stiffened.

"You two know him well?" she said.

"Yes," said Grant. "And he was missing tonight at the show. He was nowhere to be found, even missed a set."

"And before that," said Malcolm, "he'd scared the hell out of Brenna. Her car broke down and when she saw him, she ran. He grabbed her and brought her to us at the show. It was crazy."

"And the way he acted afterward, to Sharon… it was weird."

Lynne was becoming alarmed. "Did he act as if he knew Sharon?" she asked anxiously.

"No, but the thing is, she didn't act like she knew him either. And I know she's a fan. She was surprised when we called him Lance."

Lynne was confused. "How could she not know him? They were–" Lynne stopped herself short, realizing she'd started to say too much.

"They were what?" asked Grant.

Lynne tried to avoid the question and looked at her phone. "Damn," she said. "I think something is wrong. My contact should have answered by now, I texted her from the car."

"We should go," said Malcolm.

"Wait," said Grant. "She never told me what she's doing out here almost to my ranch." He then looked sternly at Lynne. "Well?" he said.

Lynne took a deep breath. She knew that Sharon and Brenna could be in some kind of trouble. And she also knew that if she wanted to get to them, she was going to have to go through these two men. She would tell them everything she knew. And had to do it fast.

# Chapter Thirty

Sharon heard her phone beep faintly several times. It was a custom notification meaning Lynne had texted her. Gus had taken their phones and purses from them and locked them in a bag by the door. She wished she had the gun she had hidden in that purse. He hadn't found it. The sound of the notification was muffled but she could hear it. Thus far, Gus had not. She hoped Lynne's instincts were as good as she thought and she would figure out that something was wrong. She didn't want her to show up unprepared. Or without reinforcements, for that matter.

Sharon had come up with a plan, however, that could give Lance and Brenna a chance to escape. All she had to do now was convince them to go along with it.

Brenna was holding her own, despite Bart's constant advances and threats. She too was thinking of a way to help the others escape. If they could hold out for just a little while longer, she would come up with a plan. She might have to risk her own life to do it, but she wouldn't give it a second thought. Meanwhile, she secretly untied Lance's wrists. He would keep his hands behind him, though, for now. He thanked her with a wink.

While Gus and Bart stood at a far window, watching for Malcolm and Grant, Sharon leaned over and began to whisper. "I have a plan to get you two out of here," she said.

Lance and Brenna immediately protested, but Sharon wouldn't hear them. "I'm going to get Bart over there to take me to the bathroom, which I really do need to use very badly!"

Lance tensed up immediately. "Absolutely not!" he warned. Brenna grabbed his arm to calm him, but neither was liking Sharon's idea.

"Just listen," Sharon insisted. "While I have him in the back, Brenna, you're going to get thirsty or something and insist that Gus let you go into the kitchen. When he heads over there to try and stop you, you'll trip, causing him to fall over you, and Lance will jump him and knock his ass out. Then you'll both get the hell out of here!"

The other two stared at her blankly for several moments before Lance belted out louder than he's intended. "What?!"

His eyes were burning into Sharon while the two women quickly looked to see if the other two men had heard him. To their relief, they hadn't.

Lance spoke again, quieter, but with the same intensity. "Have you lost your damned mind? I'm not gonna run like a coward and leave you in the hands of that over-sexed maniac!"

"Look, both of you," said Sharon. "That faint beeping means Lynne texted me. She'll know that if I'm not responding that something is wrong. I'm sure she's on her way here and I don't want her walking into a trap."

She stared at Lance with pleading eyes, begging him to see the sense in her plan. He looked at her the same way, begging her to reconsider doing it this way. But he knew her well. Once her mind was made up, there was no changing it.

"I'm not leaving you here alone and that's all there is to it," said Lance.

"I agree with you, Sharon," said Brenna, keeping an eye on the two men at the window. "We have to do something, but I also agree with Lance. We're not leaving you here alone with that creep."

"If either of you have a better plan, I'm more than happy to hear it," said Sharon. "But remember that Lynne as well as Malcolm and Grant could all be on their way here. We have to act."

Both Lance and Brenna were already worried about that, but to hear it and realize that time was ticking, made

151

them both even more anxious and ready to stop this once and for all.

They watched Gus nibbled on a piece of chicken he'd taken from the refrigerator. Sharon looked at Lance and Brenna, signaling she was ready to go on with the plan. They reluctantly nodded, letting her know they were ready too.

"Excuse me big fella," Sharon called out looking at Bart. "I need to go to the bathroom, please." She wiggled her legs as if she couldn't wait much longer.

Gus approached her first, but Bart intervened, as she suspected he would. "Sure, purdy lady, I'll be more than pleased to see you to the girls' room," he said, motioning the way down the hall.

Bart's grin made Lance's back stiffen. Sharon touched his arm gently in reassurance. Then she gave him a quick smile and left the couch. As she passed Bart, he limited her space so that she would have to brush against him as she went by. Then he turned and gave Lance a cryptic look. Lance knew this plan had to work, and quickly, for Sharon's sake.

Suddenly, a car could be heard coming up the driveway. Gus dropped the chicken leg and ran to the window. He saw a truck making its way to the house. "Hey, Bart!" Gus yelled. "Come back! Someone's here! Get ready!"

Bart raced back into the room with Sharon at his side. He gave her a shove toward the couch, as he continued

152

toward the window. "Sorry little lady. You're gonna have to hold it until we finish these two off."

Sharon and Brenna tried to think of something fast. But Lance knew what to do. He had to distract the men so the girls could run out and warn the others. Without another thought, Lance was up on his feet and barreled into the two men at the window as he shouted for the girls to run. They were stunned for a moment, but finally regained their senses and bolted for the door.

Bart was the first to recover from the blow and reached out and grabbed Sharon's leg. She fell through the front door and landed on the porch. He shoved Lance and went after Sharon who was scrambling to her feet. But soon his massive arms were around her waist as he lifted her up and pulled her back into the house. Brenna had made it and was running toward the truck.

Once inside, Bart saw that Gus had managed to knock Lance unconscious with the butt of a gun. He told him he needed to get the other girl and anyone else who was out there. When Gus ran through the door, he saw that Brenna had changed directions and was running away from the truck that had stopped.

Gus ran to the truck with his gun pointed and ready to fire, but the truck was empty. There was no one in sight, so he rushed after Brenna.

"Okay little lady. It's just you and ol' Bart now." Bart started down the hallway with Sharon still in his clutches. "Now you be nice," he said, "and you can live a long life…

at least 'til I get bored with ya." Then he threw her onto Grant's bed. "Who knows, I might not get bored with ya. You might just tame ol' Bart."

"You listen to me," Sharon warned. "I'm a federal agent. Anything you do to harm me will be a federal offense."

"Oh, I've committed federal offenses before, and I think this one'll be worth it."

Then Sharon had a revelation. Gus was not the murderer at all. It was Bart! Gus could've killed them earlier, but he didn't. Instead, he'd given them ice packs and even told Brenna he hadn't meant to hit her that hard. The more she thought about it, the more Gus didn't seem to fit the profile of the person who'd beaten, raped, and murdered those women.

"It was you, wasn't it?" she said to Bart.

He just stood still with a sinister grin on his lips and let her talk.

"You did it all, didn't you? It wasn't Gus. If he was the killer, he would've killed us when he had the chance. Tonight, he kept stopping you when you tried to hurt us, and he didn't kill Brenna when he picked her up in the field. He took her to Malcolm instead. But I'll bet he thinks he killed Jill. And you've held it over his head and made him do things he wouldn't have done otherwise."

Bart wrenched his hands together in silence, waiting patiently for her to become quiet. Until she made one last remark.

"What do you think he'll do to you when he finds out that you killed Jill and made him think he'd done it?"

Bart's face turned to a demonic one.

"Well, well, well," he said. "The government's finest at work," he sneered and advanced toward her, causing her to back up against the wall.

"What can I say? You got me. Yeah, I killed her. She'd promised herself to me, forsaking my brother and anyone else. He just didn't know it yet. When Gus and I saw her with that big biker, Malcolm, I had to teach her a lesson." He gave Sharon's body a long, lingering stare.

"After Gus fled the room, thinking he'd killed her, I went in there with her. She hurt my pride," he said. "Laughed in my face. Even called me and my brother stupid cowboys. I showed her how stupid this cowboy was. Then I had to help Gus get back at Malcolm."

He slowly crawled onto the bed and when his face was within inches of hers, he said, "Oh, how I would've enjoyed you. But my brother must never know the truth, so it's time to say goodbye."

Sharon screamed as he reached for her throat.

# Chapter Thirty-One

Headlights off, Grant and Malcolm had driven to a point on the ranch where they could view the house and surroundings for anything out of the ordinary. Lynne had followed. The three of them had come to the realize that the Lance they'd seen over the last couple of days might have been an imposter. He'd never looked at them directly, and his face was always partly covered. And with Sharon not recognizing him, they had to seriously consider their theory was true.

When they saw that all the lights were off in the house and an unfamiliar car was tucked in the trees, they made a plan. They left Lynne's car and rode in the truck to the driveway. Once there, Malcolm and Lynne climbed out and Grant drove up the driveway. He stopped at a point just beside some tall prairie grass so he could slip out unseen, but close enough to the house for the truck to be heard and seen. He left the headlights on to give the allusion the truck was still occupied.

When they saw one man run after Brenna and another grab Sharon, they split up. Lynne followed swiftly as Grant ran to the house. Lynne peered in with her gun cocked and saw nothing at first. Then there was a groan. It was Lance, just regaining consciousness. Then they heard Sharon scream, and Grant didn't waste another second. He ran through the house until he found her.

"Sharon!" he yelled when he reached his bedroom and saw a man trying to put his hands around Sharon's throat. While fighting her attacker, she saw Grant rush toward them like a runaway train. He tore Bart from the bed and onto the floor, and began pummeling him with his fists. Seconds later, Bart was knocked out cold.

Grant left Bart's bloody body lying and ran to Sharon. They held each other tight. For both of them, fear had finally turned to relief. "Tell me you're all right," he said. "And tell me the truth."

"I'm all right, Grant. I'm all right now," she said holding him even tighter.

"I was so scared that I was too late," he said. "And when I came in here, I just lost it. I really care for you Sharon. And I want us to spend a lot more time together, if you want that too."

"Yes, I want that more than anything," she replied. "But there's so much I have to explain."

"I know you work for the FBI," he said.

Sharon was surprised and happy that he knew the truth, but she was also worried. "I want you to know that we really did meet by chance. I didn't know that you knew Malcolm when we met, and he really is my favorite wrestler."

Grant could see the concern in her eyes. He gave her a reassuring smile and stroked her hair. "I know," he said. "And I also know that there are no coincidences. We were meant to bump into each other."

He lowered his head down to hers and their lips lightly touched. Then, after looking into each other's eyes for approval, their kiss was much deeper.

Gus chased Brenna across a field and finally caught up to her. He was able to knock her to the ground, and she tried to crawl away, kicking and hitting him as he tried to grab hold of her. He laughed aloud at her feistiness, knowing her efforts would be in vain.

"Okay, it's over now," he said, pointing his gun. "Let's get back to the house. Whoever's come to rescue ya' is no doubt there by now. Let's go." Gus ushered her to get up and wondered to himself whether Bart had the house under control, or if he would have to take care of business himself. "Get moving," he said.

Brenna got to her feet and something caught her eye. When Gus turned to investigate, he came face to face with an infuriated Malcolm who knocked the gun from his hand and grabbed him by the front of his coat.

Malcolm was trembling with rage. "You dare put your hands on my woman?" Then he struck him the first time, sending the man stumbling backwards. Malcolm grabbed him again. "Now tell me what you've done with Lance!" he roared.

Brenna shouted, "Malcolm, Lance is all right! He's in the house right now!" As she scrambled to find the gun in the moonlight, Malcolm punched Gus again, sending him twirling to the ground.

When Malcolm turned around, however, Gus was able to get to his feet. He turned Malcolm around and kicked him hard in the chest.

"Yeah, Lance is safe and sound at the house," Gus said in a mocking tone. "For the moment." Then he grabbed hold of Malcolm, who was doubled over and punched him across the jaw. "You have all the balls in the world to speak to me about touching your woman." He punched him again. "Or is it just all right for you to touch other men's girlfriends, wives; hell, even mothers; I don't know what turns you on."

Malcolm backed up and tried to get his bearings and Gus stalked toward him for another attack. "But there's one little lady you never should have touched," said Gus. "That's was my Jill." With that, he kicked Malcolm again, this time firmly in the side.

"If you loved her so much," said Malcolm, barely standing and holding his side, "why did you kill her?"

Malcolm was kicked again and fell to the ground. When Gus prepared to strike him again, someone jumped on his back and was raking his eyes. He stumbled and grabbed Brenna by the arms and pulled her over his head and to the ground. "This lady likes to play rough too!" he said with enjoyment. Turning his attention to her completely, he laughed and pulled her up by the arm. And he laughed. "Standing by your man, huh? Well, you'll be lying by your man in a minute."

"I warned you before," said Malcolm, "don't you ever touch my woman."

Malcolm turned a stunned Gus to face him and punched him several times in the gut. With Gus winded, and bent over, Malcolm put his arm over Gus's neck, lifted the big man in the air and flipped him crashing backwards onto the ground. He then climbed over him and pulled his head up by the neck. He brought his fist back to give him another blow, but Gus wasn't moving, so Malcolm dropped him.

Finally, Brenna discovered the gun and ran to Malcolm. Even at this moment, Malcolm looked at her in the moonlight and was captured by how beautiful she was.

She fell into his arms. "Your, woman, huh?" she said with a smile.

"My woman," he repeated.

Brenna beckoned him to bring his mouth down to hers and they shared a passionate kiss. They felt so alive and so secure in each other's arms that neither wanted to let go, but they knew they had to get to the others.

Inside, Grant and Sharon re-joined Lance and Lynne in the living room and told them Bart was unconscious in the bedroom. Lynne had helped Lance to a chair and was checking out his wounds. "I'm all right," he said, looking up into Grant's concerned eyes.

"I'm glad," said Grant. "Really glad."

"Where are Malcolm and Brenna?" asked Lance.

Grant, realizing they hadn't made it in yet, rushed for the door. But just then, Bart entered the room.

"Okay, I've had enough of you all," he bellowed. "Every one of you, get over here, right now!"

This time, Bart was brandishing a gun, taking everyone by surprise. "It's gonna take more than your little fist to keep me down, boy," he told Grant.

Lynne considered how quickly she could reach her gun.

"I know what you're thinking, cop lady. But I wouldn't try it. Not unless you want one of these men killed now instead of later."

Then Bart turned to Sharon. "I was gonna kill you, but your boyfriend here changed my mind. I think I'll have some fun with you and make him watch."

Sharon felt Grant's muscles tense with anger, and she gripped his arm to try and settle him down. But she'd had enough. "Would anyone like to know why he tried to kill me? It was so I couldn't tell his brother what I'd learned."

162

Bart was caught off guard, just as she wanted. He tilted his head slightly, a cunning grin on his face.

"When his little brother Gus saw Malcolm and Jill together, Gus confronted her, but he didn't intend to kill her," said Sharon.

Bart wanted her to continue. It was giving him an unexpected thrill to hear her tell his secret to his captives.

"But Gus lost control and shoved her. She'd hit her head and was knocked out. He thought he'd killed her… but he hadn't. Bart had seen his brother fleeing the scene and found her stirring. She was hurt, but not so badly she couldn't insult and poke fun at Bart and his brother. You see, Bart was seeing her behind Gus's back. Her one-night-stand with Malcolm angered him, and her spiteful words sent him over the edge."

"So, Bart killed Jill," said Lynne.

"And he let his brother believe he'd done it," said Grant.

"Yes," Sharon confirmed. "Gus thinks they've been stalking Malcolm waiting for the perfect time to get him back. But all the while, Bart's been assaulting and killing all of those women."

Bart was no longer amused and he made his final move toward Sharon. "Little lady, I'm gonna enjoy this."

"I don't think you want to do that," said Malcolm in a thunderous tone.

Bart stopped in his tracks and turned to see Malcolm and Brenna appear. Malcolm had Gus in his grip and a gun pointed at his head.

"Drop the gun," Malcolm ordered. "If you care at all for your brother's life."

Bart looked at Gus with indifference. "My brother understands. Don't you, Gus?" he said smartly. While he spoke to his brother, he secretly wondered if he'd heard any of Sharon's story. He searched his expression for the answer, but Gus seemed dazed at the moment.

"So, why don't we see how much you care for your friends instead," said Bart. "What if I accidentally shoot one?"

Bart raised the gun and pointed it at Grant's head. Malcolm's heart stopped. This man didn't give a damn what happened to his brother, or anyone else. He had no other leverage. He had to give in to save Grant. He released Gus and carefully laid the gun on the floor.

"Good," said Bart. "Now Gus, pick up that gun."

Gus slowly bent down to pick it up. He still seemed staggered and weak as his brother watched him. Once he stood up with the gun, he looked over every person in the room, especially the women. Then he turned to his brother. "Let me have your gun too, Bart. I'll watch them while you get the car. Then we can get the hell out of here."

Bart gave his brother a satisfied smile. "Good thinking. But don't forget, the women are coming with us."

When Bart placed the gun in Gus's hand, Gus stood a little straighter and his eyes became dark, but Bart didn't notice. "No, Bart," he said. "The women stay here with their men. You and I have to go now."

Gus's voice was very deep and calm. That surprised Bart. He didn't understand.

"But Gus, we have to make them pay for Jill's death, remember?"

"Jill's death? Yes, big bro. Let's talk about her death. I heard everything. The two of you had a thing? You killed her, *and* you let me take the blame? And all those women… you did that too? Taking women's lives and their livelihood?" Gus was getting so worked up that he could hardly contain himself. He looked as if he would soon implode. His voice booming, he barked in his brother's face, "You're never gonna hurt anyone again. Come with me, now!"

The others in the room were all standing and worried what was about to transpire.

"Wait Gus," Bart pleaded, trying to hold his brother off with his hands and backing up. "What are you doing? We're brothers."

"You're no brother of mine," Gus spat. "You did the deeds and it's time for you to pay the piper."

Gus ushered Bart to the door and motioned for Brenna and Malcolm to get out of the way.

Bart protested the entire way, but Gus was an unyielding force pressing him on. Bart suddenly ran out the door and Gus went after. Three shots were heard by the others. Everyone else hit the floor, but Lynne inched to the door with her gun and Sharon crept behind, keeping low. They heard a car fire up. A body was lying on the dirt when the car sped away.

Lynne went to the body, lying some feet away. She gave Sharon the nod that Bart was dead. After the speeding car was out of ear shot, Sharon turned and sat on the floor against the door frame. "Bart's dead," she breathed.

Lynne came back up the porch steps and helped Sharon stand up. The others gathered around.

"Gus got away," said Lynne.

"Yeah, he did, didn't he?"

They both looked out at the road, seeing nothing and no one.

"What do you think we should do about it?" Sharon asked as they watched the dust settle.

"He did save our lives," said Brenna.

"More than once," said Sharon.

"His brother was the only killer," said Lynn. "And I'll say this was self-defense."

"And he didn't even know his brother was involved those attacks," said Brenna. "He thought they were just planning revenge against Malcolm. He was in anguish over thinking he'd killed Jill, and he couldn't forgive himself. Bart used that anguish to his own advantage. He wanted him to kill Malcolm."

"But I don't think he could've gone through with it," said Lance. "Trust me, I got to know them both real' good, real' fast," he said, rubbing his jaw. "And Gus was tormented by something. Deep down he knew his brother was doing wrong, and he couldn't stand up to him."

Malcolm and Grant agreed with Lance, and the three women agreed that Gus was just another victim and that's how their reports would read.

"Well, ladies, what now?" asked Grant, putting his arm around Sharon.

"Case closed," the women said happily in unison.

Afterward, the three couples went on to live happy lives together, putting all of this behind them. But then, that's another story.

# Epilogue

A grueling day had just come to an end, and so had a three-month storyline. Malcolm was finally home for an extended stay and was exhausted. His thoughts were of Brenna during his flight. For some reason he hadn't been able to contact her, which concerned him. Since they'd started dating exclusively, they had always been able to reach each other.

He entered his house, dropping his baggage at the door, and ascended the stairs to his bedroom. He went straight for the bathroom. A nice, hot, soothing shower would do the body some good.

As he disrobed, his mind wandered back to the time in Phoenix when he was in the shower and Brenna surprised him by joining him. As much as he delighted in the possibilities, he knew it wasn't the right time or place.

But if it were now, he would be more than willing to fulfill her every fantasy.

He stepped into the shower, allowing the hot steaming water to flow down his long loose hair and over his tight muscles. His mind wandered once again to thoughts of having his lady love there to share this moment with him. He thought of what he would do if she were there. Then he felt the brush of a small body against him, and arms moving around his waist. He swirled around, thinking his imagination had taken a life of its own; but it was not so. He stared into those sensual eyes.

"Brenna," he said happily.

"We have some unfinished business," she said.

She took his face into her hands and pulled him to her, and she claimed his mouth with hers.

He held her tighter in his arms. The kiss was the prelude of sweeter things to come. He lifted her up and backed her against the wall; she wrapped her legs around him. He entered her gently, connecting them as one. They moved in unison, each fueling the other with pure animal energy, until each had given all they could in a fervent release. Brenna screamed in ecstasy and went limp in his arms.

Malcolm growled satisfactorily and stepped out of the shower, carrying her into the bedroom. He laid Brenna on the bed and lay at her side. She turned to face him and they stared into the other's eyes. "I'm glad you finally used that key I gave to you," he said.

"Surprised?" she asked.

"Yes. And I was worried when I couldn't reach you."

"I apologize," she said. "I was caught up in trying to get here before you."

"Oh, so you got here before me?" he laughed.

"Do you remember that night on the hill, when I wanted you but you wouldn't?" asked Brenna.

"Yes, I do," he answered. "I wanted you, but not like that. I wanted you in my home and in my bed."

"But it didn't happen that way our first time," she said.

"That's because I had to show you that there wasn't anything you had to fear from me," said Malcolm.

"I know," she said and went deep into thought. She remembered that day, and how tender and affectionate he'd been.

"You know that I love you," he said.

"Yes," said Brenna happily. "I've known ever since that day."

"Well, we're here, in my home and in my bed," he grinned wickedly.

He moved slowly over her body and captured her wanting lips with his. They were joined once again, their silhouettes on the wall mimicked their every move. The air filled with the sounds of the enjoyment each received from the other. She moaned from the feel of him; he was her match.

He loved how her walls caressed him, intensifying his movement. When their lovemaking reached its climax, their passion flowed freely, sending them to heights neither had ever reached before. Then, slowly, they relaxed in each other's arms, weakened, fulfilled, and full of love.

No more would he have to get past the deed with the mystery woman of his dreams. She was there in reality, forever. Next, he would ask her to be his wife.

# Also by S.R. Burks

For more about these and other titles,
visit the official website of the author:
www.SRBurks.com.

For more from Nocturna Press, visit
www.NocturnaPress.com.